"We can't sleep together . . ."

Jenna's voice shook as she attempted to set some ground rules. "I mean, we can't spend the *whole* night together in my bedroom."

Spence looked displeased. "Why not?"

"This is a business arrangement." Her gaze searched his. "It wouldn't be right."

He frowned. "But I was looking forward to having a warm body next to me. And what if we want to have sex more than once? Am I supposed to run back and forth down the hall?"

"We can't do it more than once a night. My doctor says so. You'd be, uh, continually depleted. . . ."

Spence grinned. "*Some* men might be depleted, but when I get going . . ."

"Please, Spence. We're trying to make a baby. It's not as if we're in love, is it?"

Readers have nothing but praise for **Barbara Delinsky**, popular author of over fifty novels. And no wonder! Barbara's stories are always emotional, sexy and poignant. This Massachusetts native also likes to be controversial, as in *The Stud*. Jenna, the heroine, will do *anything* to have a baby— something women in the nineties can identify with, Barbara says. This talented writer is already working on her next Temptation novel, which features a very unusual hero.

Books by Barbara Delinsky

HARLEQUIN TEMPTATION

Don't miss any of our special offers. Write to us at the following address for information on our newest releases.

- Harlequin Reader Service
P.O. Box 1397, Buffalo, NY 14240
Canadian address: P.O. Box 603,
Fort Erie, Ont. L2A 5X3

The Stud
BARBARA DELINSKY

Harlequin Books

TORONTO • NEW YORK • LONDON
AMSTERDAM • PARIS • SYDNEY • HAMBURG
STOCKHOLM • ATHENS • TOKYO • MILAN

Published August 1991

ISBN 0-373-25457-1

THE STUD

1

IT WAS THE SCAR that scraped along his jaw that was so compelling.

No, it was his hair. Dark and windblown, it lent him a look that held more than a hint of the rogue.

Then again, it had to be his eyes. They radiated from the photograph, silver-blue and electric, which was startling since the photograph was black and white. But Jenna McCue had seen those eyes in person, and once seen, they were never forgotten.

Feeling oddly as though they'd touched her even then, she flipped the book over to bury the back-cover photograph in the seat of the car, which left the front cover staring up at her. *Green Gold* was the title of the book. The story inside dealt with the search for emeralds in the mines of South Africa, and it was a true story. Spencer Smith had lived through the adventure and written about it just as he had written about his search for treasure in the shadow of the pyramids in Egypt, in the Peruvian Andes, in pirate coves of the South Seas. His books weren't best-sellers. They lacked the requisite elements for commercial success, namely melodrama and sex. Rather, they were well-written documentaries, sure to fascinate the adventurer-at-heart.

Jenna wasn't quite that, since her life was ruled by routine, but Spencer Smith was the brother of her oldest and dearest friend. She would have bought his books out of loyalty to Caroline and her family, even if she hadn't found them intriguing. But she loved each one. Over the years, she had become the unofficial, if biased, reviewer of his books on her visits with the Smiths.

This visit had a different purpose, though. True, she had read and loved *Green Gold,* and true, she wouldn't have missed the senior Smiths' fiftieth wedding anniversary party for the world, but she had more on her agenda than drinking champagne, eating lobster and waltzing across the dance floor with whoever chose to ask her to dance.

She had something to ask of Spencer Smith. A favor of sorts. A proposition of sorts. A personal, *very* personal request. An unusual one, for sure.

He might be incredulous or mocking, intrigued or repulsed. Caroline had suggested all those things by way of preparing Jenna for the worst, but she had agreed with Jenna's idea, and rightfully so. It was a good one. From the moment she'd thought of it, Jenna had known that it made perfect sense. It would satisfy a number of people on a number of different scores. All she had to do was to convince Spencer of that.

Turning onto the private lane that led to the Smiths' Newport home, she pulled up behind the last car in line, climbed out and set off toward the house. Her heels were pale yellow and high, not ideal for walking over a dirt road, but they went with her dress, which was silk with a short skirt and matching jacket, and the entire look went with her hair, which was loosely curled and feminine. Normally she dressed more sleekly and knotted her hair back, as befitted a top-level executive. But even aside from the occasion of the Smiths' party, she was feeling softer.

It had to do with where she was in life and what she wanted in her future, which was where Spencer came in. Ignoring the gentle curling in the pit of her stomach, she walked on.

The closer she came to the house, the more people she saw. She recognized several and offered warm hellos, then was quickly introduced to others, and while those others might not have known her on sight, by reputation they did. McCue's was a venerable name in New England retailing. The McCue chain of department stores, falling somewhere in style between Bergdorf Goodman and Jordan Marsh, had survived good times and bad to become the stalwart outlet to which New Englanders went for everything from polo shirts and jeans to suede suits, sterling-silver picture frames and designer bed coverings. Jenna, as the last living McCue, was president and chairman of the board. At thirty-five, she was an effective and insightful leader. As her father and her grandfather before him had done, she kept the store apace with the times, which was why McCue's thrived while others felt the economy's pinch. She anticipated problems and dealt with them before they became debilitating in any way, shape or form.

She did the same with her personal life, which was why she had to talk with Spencer.

He wasn't in the foyer when she entered the house, or in the living room when she passed through on her way to the patio, where Joe and Abby Smith were accepting congratulations from their guests. Jenna gave them both affectionate hugs and chatted for several minutes before moving on to allow other guests access. She had barely taken a glass of wine from a passing tray, when Caroline materialized beside her.

"You look spectacular," she said, giving Jenna a prolonged once-over before adding a dubious, "did I see that dress at the store?"

Jenna glanced around casually to make sure no one was within earshot. There were perks to her profession, but she wasn't one to broadcast them. Sotto voce she admitted, "We ordered a few at the Paris show, then decided they'd be too pricey to carry in quantity. I took one of the few. Like it?"

"You know I do, but whether I'm more envious of the dress or your figure, I'm not sure. You're so slim. Lord, what I'd give to be a size six."

Jenna sent her a meaningful look. "Lord, what I'd give to have three kids." Her eyes searched the crowd. "Where are they?"

"Somewhere out there. I told Annie to watch Wes and Wes to watch Nathan, so the three should be running after one another all afternoon. I'm assuming someone else will notice if one of them falls into the pool."

"They're super kids," Jenna said, and meant it, though her eyes weren't at kid level as they continued to roam the crowd.

"He's not here yet," Caroline told her. "He called a while ago to say he'd run into thunderstorms over D.C. and had to detour to Pittsburgh for fuel. He says he's flying into Newport State. I wouldn't put it past him to land on our beach."

"He wouldn't."

The look Caroline sent her said that he very well would, and, giving it a second thought, Jenna didn't argue. For anyone other than Spencer Smith, landing on the rocky beach rimming Rhode Island Sound would be suicidal. But Spencer had a way of courting danger and emerging alive. Jenna supposed he could successfully land his Cessna on that narrow strip of sand, taxi up to the dock and step out of the cabin totally unruffled.

He was a strong man. He was an able man. He was a man with a natural curiosity, who wasn't afraid to ask questions or tackle the unknown. There were some who, in moments of sheer envy, called him a fool for taking the chances he did. But Jenna had read his books and knew that the opposite was true. As hare-brained as some of his escapades might appear on the surface, he never did anything without weighing the odds and ensuring that they were tipped in his favor. In that sense, he was extraordinarily intelligent.

Intelligent. Competent. Strong. Curious. Courageous. All were fine qualities, ones that Jenna admired, ones that a child of hers would have, if she had any say in the matter.

"He'll get here," Caroline said with a reassuring squeeze.

"But will he stay long enough for us to talk? I need privacy for this. It isn't the kind of question one pops with a zillion people listening in."

"He says he's staying through the weekend."

"He's said that before and then taken off. He has trouble sitting still."

"Only with his family. Set him up on the shores of Loch Ness, and he'll sit motionless for days waiting for the monster to surface. Newport makes him nervous. *We* make him nervous. He's convinced that the one thing we want most in life is to break him to a saddle." Caroline laughed. "As if we could." A second laugh turned into a groan. "What was that?"

Jenna had seen it, too, the streaking of a three-year-old child through the gathering of guests. "Looked like Nathan."

"Looked like wedding cake," Caroline muttered. "I'll kill him." With a murderous look, she was off.

Jenna watched her go, feeling both affection and envy. Then she took a deep breath and released it. Spencer wasn't there. He wouldn't arrive for a while. She could relax.

For the next two hours, she did just that. She liked the Smiths' friends, many of whom were her own, and socializing was second nature to her. Like Caroline, she had been raised in the lap of luxury. Her parents had had money to spare, and though they had loved traveling and eating out and donating hospital wings in their name, more than anything they had loved parties. From the earliest Jenna could remember, they were either throwing one or attending one. Out of sheer survival, Jenna had learned to mix, and though she had never developed the love for loud festivities that her parents had, she had come to be perfectly at ease. The key, she knew, was to smile, to indulge in amiable small talk, to read other people's needs and listen or respond accordingly—without taking any of it seriously. Gossip never touched her. One part of her remained removed from it all and therefore protected.

She munched on the food that was first passed on silver trays, then offered in a lavish sit-down buffet. She chatted and laughed. She raised her glass when Caroline's husband, a state representative with a golden tongue, proposed a toast to his in-laws, and she couldn't help but think that Spencer should have been the one to do that. But he wouldn't have. Not even if he'd come on time. As adventurous as the man was, he wasn't a showman. As compelling as he was, he shunned the limelight. While another man in his shoes would have brought a film crew along on his trips, Spencer refused. He was determined to enjoy adventure for adventure's sake. If a book came later, fine. If the book was spiced up and made into a movie, that was fine, too. He would serve as a technical consultant, but that was all.

Spencer's toast wasn't missed. There were plenty of others, offered by various and sundry of the Smiths' friends and relatives, to the extent that the guests ceased to sit between toasts. Even then, when Spencer appeared on the outskirts of the crowd, Jenna saw him at once. He was that kind of man. Standing six-foot-four, he was taller than most others in the room, but that wasn't what did it, as much as his aura. Complemented by his roguishly dark good looks and the confidence of his stance, he exuded independence, self-containment and, while not quite disdain, a disinclination to play games by any rules other than his own.

Jenna hadn't seen Spencer for six years, yet she felt his force at once. It was far stronger than anything she'd encountered on the back of a book jacket and it gave her a moment's pause. She wasn't sure she could approach him. He was so . . . *much*. And she'd never been terribly good with men in anything but business.

But this *was* business, she reminded herself, and with that thought stilled her wildly beating heart. She couldn't take her eyes from him, though, but watched him take in the situation and back off. He would wait, she knew, until the toasts were done. In the flurry of movement when people returned to their seats, he would slip into his own at his parents' table.

That was what he did. Slowly word spread that he was there, and though no one dared raise a glass to the success of *Green Gold,* those closest to the family made a point of going over to greet the author. The rest kept their distance, and wisely so. Spencer had never been the kiss-kiss type. His silver-blue eyes were legendary in their ability to cut phonies down with a glance.

Jenna, too, kept her distance, though not from fear of being cut down. As Caroline's friend, she had immunity. Spencer had always been kind to her, even gentle, just as he was to his sister. For whatever differences he had with his parents, Caroline was special to him. He never failed to call her on her birthday or to send a gift to one of her children on theirs. Jenna respected him for that. She also took it as a clue to his character, a part of him few people saw. She was counting on the clue being apt.

No, it wasn't fear of Spencer that kept Jenna from rushing up to him, as much as a desire to carefully control her approach. Her mission was a delicate one. She wanted to maximize her chance of success. Or so she told herself. But long after the band started playing and people had moved onto the dance floor, she hung back. She immersed herself in conversation with people who stood at the greatest distance from Spencer. She walked Annie, Wes and Nathan down to the beach when she was sure Spencer was with followers in the gazebo. She finally agreed to Charleston with an old family friend, but quickly moved off into the crowd and oblivion the instant the dance was done. When coffee was served and a tiered wedding cake rolled onto the lawn, minus several frosting roses that small fingers had filched, she clung to the fringes.

Her time would come, she knew. When the guests had left and things had quieted, Spencer would be feeling mellow. A mellow Spencer would be more approachable than one whose defenses were in place. A mellow Spencer would be more disposed to consider her proposal. A mellow Spencer would be more likely to accept.

But a mellow Spencer wasn't what she got when, with the party still in full swing, she felt a commanding hand on her arm. She barely had time to look around when, in his deep, brooking-no-defiance voice, Spencer told those with whom she'd been talking, "Would you excuse Jenna? I need her help with something."

Neither expecting, wanting nor waiting for permission, he drew her free of the circle. His large hand circled hers as he led her off.

"Spencer?" she asked.

But his attention was on working his way through the crowd. "Excuse us," he said, and slid through one narrow opening, then wove through another. "Sorry. Excuse us. Thanks."

Jenna didn't bother to say his name again. The set of his jaw told her that he was tense. She didn't want to antagonize him, when she had such a delicate favor to ask. So she went where he led, knowing that he would explain himself in time.

Indeed, as soon as they had cleared the gathering of people on the lawn, he said, "Walk with me. I need air."

Glad to be of help, she walked. From time to time, she trotted to make up a step on his longer stride, and by the time they reached the end of the lawn, where the retaining wall was broken by steps to the beach, the huff of his pace had eased.

"Can you handle the sand?" he asked with a glance at her shoes.

Using his arm for balance, she slipped off one, then the other of the pale yellow heels. He pushed them into his blazer pockets before she could protest the abuse of the fine cloth, and in the next breath, he pulled the tie from his neck and crammed it in with one of the shoes in a way that said he didn't care.

"You do know that it's painful for me to watch that," she teased, holding her hair back from her face, where the shore breeze seemed intent on blowing it.

The look he sent her was dark, but indulgently so. "You're Caroline's friend. You'll forgive me." Taking her hand again, he led her down the steps to the beach, along the narrow boardwalk that had been laid years before as a concession to the sharp pebbles, to the far dock. He didn't stop until they were at its very edge. Stepping out of his shoes—Jenna wasn't at all surprised that he hadn't worn socks—he tugged her down to sit beside him.

She gave a brief thought to the silk skirt that was sure to be bruised on the weathered plants—but only a brief thought. One skirt, silk or otherwise, was nothing compared to Spencer's good favor. One skirt was nothing compared to her future.

She wasn't sure why, but he continued to hold her hand. Since the feeling wasn't unpleasant, she let it be.

The tide was out. Their legs dangled a good eight feet above the water, which lapped softly at the rocks on the shore behind them. From a distance came the muted tinkle of a bell buoy. Both sounds were gentle, far more so than Spencer's expression as he stared across the sound.

"Things like this try me," he said after a long, brooding minute.

"Parties?"

"They're so excessive."

"But they give your parents pleasure."

"Does that justify the waste?"

With a sigh, Jenna faced the water. She wasn't going to argue with him.

"You think it does?" he challenged.

Gently she said, "Not personally, no. I lean toward moderation. But what's right for me may not be right for someone else. Your parents are like mine were. They're social creatures, and they have the money. If they want to spend it on a party, that's their choice. As long as they don't tell me how to live my life, I can let them live theirs."

Spencer shifted her hand from the small space between them to his thigh. He studied her fingers, which were absurdly pale and slender between his long, tanned ones.

"I won't run away," she said quietly.

He shot her a solemn look that was binding, given the silver of his eyes. "I wasn't sure of that. You've been doing your best to avoid me all afternoon."

"All afternoon?" She tugged a strand of hair away from her mouth. "You haven't been here but half of it."

"Thank the good Lord for that," he muttered. He released another button—the third—on his shirt, filled his lungs with the tangy salt air and blew it out along, it seemed to Jenna, with a bit of his tension. His voice was as deep as ever but less tight. "I have trouble enough with my parents alone. With two hundred of their friends, I'm in pain."

"This from a man who once stood bound to a stake waiting to be boiled for dinner by a bunch of cannibals?"

"You've been reading too much," he grumbled.

"I like your books."

"So does Hollywood. *Green Gold* has been optioned for another Indiana Jones type of thing."

"That's great!"

"I'm not so sure. It takes away from my credibility. Treasure hunting is serious stuff."

"Yes," Jenna said with due graveness. "I can tell that from your books."

He looked at her.

"I can," she insisted.

"Mmm." Neither taking a breath nor looking away, he said, "Caroline told me you wanted to talk."

Jenna's heart fell. She hadn't wanted Caroline to say anything. She had wanted to pick the time herself, and this wasn't it. If Spencer had felt strangled at the party, this *definitely* wasn't it. She wanted him to be feeling loose and open to suggestion when she hit him with her request.

"It can wait," she said lightly.

"Caroline said it was important. Twice she told me that."

"She shouldn't have."

"It's not important?"

"It is, but there's no urgency to it. We should probably be going back to the party, anyway."

"I don't want to go back to the party."

"But it's your parents' fiftieth anniversary. That's a precious milestone."

"Uh-huh, and I invited them to celebrate with me in the Keys, but they refused."

"Because they're party people. They wanted *everyone* with them." Her curiosity got the best of her. "What are you doing in the Keys?" With his hair blowing in the breeze, his shirt agape to mid-chest and the scar slashing his jaw, she imagined him a pirate.

"Waiting for a court to decide whether I have the exploration rights to a site where a Spanish galleon sank in the eighteenth century."

Her eyes widened. "You've found the galleon?"

He nodded. "One of my divers, the first one to spot the wreck, took off and formed his own salvage crew and is claiming that the rights to explore it are his. Neither of us can touch it until the court acts, and the court is pathetically slow. Another six weeks and we'll be into the hurricane season. No one will be doing any exploring then until late fall."

She gathered her windblown hair in her free hand. "Is there gold on the boat?"

"If the boat turns out to be the one I think and if my research is correct, there is. There should also be a wealth of artifacts aboard."

"Perfectly preserved?" she asked. She was always in awe of the fact that things could emerge from the ocean floor intact after hundreds of years. There seemed something incredibly peaceful about that, which was ironic given the tumult of a shipwreck.

"Some things will be preserved. Others may have to be restored."

"Is this your next book?"

"If the court rules in my favor. If not, I'm out one adventure."

"You'll find another. You always do. How do you manage it?"

"I have friends in strange places. They tip me off."

"You network," she said with a smile at the term, which she never would have thought to apply to treasure hunting before.

"I suppose." He flattened her hand on his thigh and imprisoned it there. "What did you want to ask me?"

"Later." She could feel the heat and hardness of muscle, and tried to extract her hand, but he refused to let go.

"I may not be here later."

"Oh, Spencer. You told Caroline you'd stay through tomorrow." Again she tried to pull her hand free of his touch, this time as a gesture matching her complaint, but he held it fast.

"That was before I came."

"You've only been here two hours."

"And already I'm choking."

"Oh, dear," Jenna said before she could help herself, because if he felt like he was choking, the *last* thing she could do was to jump into a discussion as sensitive as the one she had in mind.

"You'd better take the chance while you have it," he warned.

"Why not when the party's done? Things will be quieter then."

He looked around. "Things are quiet now."

She let her free hand fall to her lap. The wind promptly dove into her hair, creating a veil of haphazard waves to protect her from his gaze. The next thing she knew, Spencer was gathering the long curls behind one ear and securing them with what felt suspiciously like his necktie. Left with nothing to hide behind, she looked up at him. His eyes were compellingly blue and heart-stoppingly direct. "Go ahead," he said, and captured her hand again. "I'm waiting."

Jenna's heart skipped a beat. *The time isn't right. The setting isn't right. He'll think I'm crazy. He'll say no.*

But his eyes wouldn't let up. They held her in a grip so firm that try as she might, she couldn't look away. His voice didn't help. It was deep and rich, part command, part dare. "Tell me now, Jenna. What is it you want?"

"A baby!" she cried. "I want a baby!"

2

JENNA HADN'T INTENDED to blurt it out that way, but once she'd heard the words, she knew there was no turning back. She couldn't hem and haw. She couldn't show doubt. If she was to win Spencer's cooperation, she had to make her case well.

To that end, she straightened her back, leveled her voice and said with calmness and just a touch of pride, "I want a baby. I've been wanting one for a while, but suddenly I'm thirty-five, and time's running out. The problem, obviously, is that I don't have a husband—and I don't want one," she hastened to add, lest Spencer think she wanted him for that. "I'm single by choice. I wouldn't dream of marrying just for the sake of having a baby. That could be disastrous all the way around."

Spencer was looking puzzled, something she'd never seen before. She would have laughed at the incongruity of the expression on his face if the situation wasn't so serious. Slipping her hand from beneath his, she tucked it into her lap, cleared her throat and went on.

"I've been thinking about this for a long time. I've looked at it from every angle. I've gone through all the possibilities—"

Spencer broke in, sounding as confused as he looked and oddly helpless. "You want me to help you find a baby? I know that adopting foreign kids is in, but Lord, Jenna, that's not my thing. Sure, I'm abroad all the time, but there aren't many babies in the places I hang out."

"That's not what I want."

He frowned. "Then what is?"

She had practiced the speech so many times that she knew it by heart. Granted, Spencer's interruptions might shift around the order of things, but she was determined to get it all out. "Adoption is terrific for people who can't have children of their own, but I can. I'm perfectly healthy. I've been seeing a doctor who says I shouldn't have trouble conceiving."

"Is he volunteering to help you?"

"Yes," she said, thinking in medical terms until Spencer's faint leer stopped her short. "Not in *that* sense. He's willing to help me with artificial insemination, which, as I see it, is a viable solution to the problem."

"Artificial insemination?"

"You know, where—"

"I know what it is. I just can't believe you want to go in for it. In fact, I can't believe you have this problem at all. There must be scads of men out there who'd marry you in a minute."

"Yes," she acknowledged, holding her chin firm.

"But?"

"I said it before. To marry just to have a baby is absurd. I'd marry for love, but since love hasn't hit me in the face—"

"Don't you date?"

"Some."

"And you've never felt compatible enough with any of those guys to talk about having a child together?"

"None of them fitted the bill for what I want in the father of my child."

"Are we talking stellar genes here?"

"Stellar?" She averted her eyes from his. "I suppose. I'd be a fool not to be talking that. What woman wouldn't want the father of her child to be brilliant and handsome and healthy and tall and athletic—"

"I get the point," Spencer cut in dryly.

"Mmm." She took a breath and regrouped. Looking over the sound, which was more soothing than meeting Spencer's probing eyes, she said, "I want the best for my baby. Kids nowadays have enough to face without having to worry about inborn deficiencies. I've looked into using a sperm bank."

"A sperm bank."

She kept her gaze on the water. "In theory, I could find a donor with all or most of the traits I want for my child."

"A sperm bank," Spencer repeated in a drone that brought her head around.

"I know you think the idea is ludicrous. Caroline said you might, but the fact is that it's done all the time. There's an increasing number of women in my position, wanting babies but for one reason or another not having a father for the child. That's one of the purposes of sperm banks. That's why artificial insemination has evolved into a science from an art."

He looked as though he wanted to laugh but was controlling the urge. "Artificial insemination is fine. So are sperm banks, but I still can't imagine why you'd want to use either. Come to think of it, I can't imagine why you weren't married years ago. You're pretty and smart and rich."

"Right," she drawled, "I'm rich, which means that some men would marry me just for that. I've had men tell me they loved me, when what they really meant was that they loved what I owned."

"They don't all mean that. Some of them must be sincere. You're a nice person, Jenna. You're easy on the eyes and on the mind. If I stayed put long enough, I could fall in love with you myself."

She took his comment lightly, as it had been offered. "But you won't stay put long enough, which is why you're just right."

His face went blank. For an instant, the only sounds were the water on the rocks, the bell buoy's jingle and the cry of a gull. Then he said, "Back up. You lost me."

Embarrassed that she had let the punch line slip before she should have, Jenna complained, "That's because you keep interrupting me. Will you let me take this step by step, Spencer? Let me say my *thing?*"

"Okay." He straightened. "Say your thing."

He seemed suddenly so much taller sitting beside her, that she felt foolish and insecure and presumptuous. She was *sure* Spencer wouldn't do what she wanted. He had his own life. If he wanted to father a child, he would have already found a way to do it. He was resourceful.

Resourcefulness. Another trait she admired. Another trait she would wish for in a child of hers.

Taking courage from that thought, she went on. "I'm perfectly comfortable with the idea of artificial insemination. Some woman inseminate themselves—"

"How?"

"With a syringe. Please let me go on?"

"Go on."

"I've decided to work with a doctor because the chances of success are greater. The problem is that I'm not comfortable with the idea of going to a sperm bank. I don't trust numbers on lists, and I don't care how many safeguards there are, I'd still worry that I'd get the wrong donor. Either that, or that the donor would have lied and wouldn't have half the qualities he claimed."

"Are you looking for an Einstein?"

"Spencer, please."

"Sorry. Go on."

"I'm looking for the best I can get, but there are some things a sperm bank won't tell you. They'll screen for sexually transmitted diseases, but they have no way of knowing whether one is contracted between the time of screening and the donation. They'll screen for physical traits and genetic abnormalities, but not personality traits. They won't tell you what the donor's parents or grandparents or siblings are like, and I think that's important information. Besides, sperm is usually frozen for storage in a bank, but a certain percentage of it is lost in the process. For that reason, fresh sperm is better."

Spencer was studying her in a way that would have made her squirm if she hadn't been determined to look confident. She had a feeling he sensed where she was leading. He was quick—another thing she liked about him. So she hurried on.

"I want artificial insemination, but I don't want to go to a sperm bank. The only option that's left is to find someone I know to donate his sperm, but most of the men I know are totally unsuited to the cause. Some of them would want to get married, and I don't want to do that. Some of them would want to take part in the raising of the child, and I don't want that, either. Some of them would sue for visitation rights, but when I think of my child going off with strange grandparents, I shudder. I can't think of any man around here whose family I respect enough to feel comfortable with that. Except you."

Spencer stared at her. After a minute, he said, "Go on."

"I want your sperm."

He stared harder. "You're kidding."

She shook her head. "I'm dead serious," she said with a fragment of breath. She was holding the rest, waiting for his full reaction.

"You want my sperm." It was more an echo than a question. She was sure she heard disbelief, which was better than dismay or revulsion. "How, uh, did you plan on obtaining my sperm?"

More than any other part of her speech, she had thought this part out the most carefully. She didn't want to offend a man who was as blatantly virile as Spencer Smith. Sounding as clinical as possible, she said, "My doctor has a standard procedure for this. I'd be tracking my basal body temperature to determine the exact time of ovulation. When that time comes, you'd go to his office, be given a clean container and the privacy of your own room. When you were done, you'd give him the sample and leave."

"I'd—" He made a gesture with his hand that was simultaneously obscene and accurate.

She refused to blush. "That's right."

His expression darkened. "I'd go into my own little room, lock my own little door, dream my own little dream and—"

"It wouldn't be so bad, Spencer."

"It'd be awful!"

"Men give sperm samples all the time. Remember *The Right Stuff*?"

"This isn't the movies. It's real life."

"And it's done all the time in real life. Sperm donors do it. So do men who are having fertility tests."

"So do perverts and gays and guys who can't find a woman, but I don't fit into any of those slots." He paused. When he turned his blue eyes on her this time, she felt the current down to her toes. "Why me, Jenna?"

She took a steadying breath. This was the easy part, and not only because he had to like what she said. But she believed every word, which meant that she could put her heart and soul into the argument. Turning sideways on the dock to face him more fully, she said, "Because you're right physically. You're tall and good-looking. You're intelligent and coordinated and healthy. You have all the traits I'd look for in a donor from a sperm bank, only with you I'd know the unknowns, too. I know your parents and love them. I know your sister and love her. I know that there aren't any genetic defects running through your family. I know that you have a temper but that you're perfectly sane and reasonable, and even if I don't agree with the way you deal with your parents, I admire your determination and consistency, and when it comes to a sense of adventure, you have it over everyone else hands down—" She stopped only because she'd run out of breath. As soon as she filled her lungs again, she rushed on.

"Don't you see, Spencer? Everything else is right, too. I don't want a husband—you don't want to get married. I don't want a man around—and you're never here. You don't want to play father—and I don't want to share my child. We're *both* rich, so neither of us would take advantage of the other. Think about it. This could solve your problem, too."

"What problem?"

"Your parents. They're dying for another grand-child, a child of yours this time." She knew the elder Smiths well. "Don't tell me they didn't mention it in the short time you've spent with them today." The look on his face was as good as a confession. She pressed her advantage. "They drive you *nuts* pushing for marriage and kids, but you don't want either. You don't want to be tied down. This way you could have your cake and eat it, too. You could have the child, which would please your parents and get them off your back, and you wouldn't have to give up a drop of your freedom."

Spencer stared at her for another minute before pushing a hand through his hair. A moment later, the wind mussed it again. A moment after that, he got to his feet.

"Where are you going?" she cried. There was more she wanted to say. She scrambled to her feet.

"I have to move."

Determinedly she moved right along with him. "You haven't said no. Are you considering it?"

"I'm trying to decide whether I should." He strode back along the dock with a loafer in each hand. "It's bizarre, what you're asking."

"Not bizarre. Just unusual."

"There's many a man who'd think you were crazy."

"But you don't, because you know me—" she launched into the next part or her argument "—and that's a plus for you. Yes, I know that you don't want to have a child, and yes, I know that if you did, you'd be perfectly capable of choosing its mother yourself, but I'd be a better mother than most, Spencer. You wouldn't go wrong from the physical standpoint. I have good hair, good skin, a good build."

"You're too short."

"Five-four isn't too short."

"It's nearly a full foot shorter than me."

"But a nice height for a woman. Would it bother you to have a daughter who's petite?"

"What about a son who's petite?" he tossed off as he left the dock for the beach.

"A son would inherit your height." She trotted a little to keep up, but she was hampered by the sharpness of the pebbles. "The only reason my height would be a problem was if we were actually lovers, but we're not. Everything would be done in the doctor's office." She hobbled over a particularly prickly stretch, then hurried to catch up. "I have no physical deformities, nor do my ancestors for three generations back. If my parents' plane hadn't crashed, they would have lived into their eighties as their parents did before them." He was lengthening the distance between them. She raised her voice to be heard. "I have perfect eyesight, perfect hearing, I can carry a tune and I played volleyball and tennis in high school."

"I saw you Charleston," Spencer called back.

She trotted two steps and limped on the third. "That's what I'm trying to tell you! I'm athletic!"

"So why can't you keep up with me now?"

Stopping dead in her tracks, she shouted, "Because I may be athletic, but the soles of my feet aren't made of leather! I haven't trained walking over beds of nails like you have! You have my *shoes*, Spencer!"

With little more than the toss of his dark head, he yelled, "Good! Then you won't go far until I get back!"

Jenna looked after him in exasperation, but that gave way to admiration as she watched him stride on. He was a striking figure. His limbs were long, lean but strong, and he moved with masculine grace and fluidity. She saw him stop and face the water. He lowered his head in thought. He glanced back at her.

For the longest time, she held his gaze, feeling its force even across dozens of yards of shoreline. Then, needing a respite, she retreated to the boardwalk to wait. He joined her there several minutes later, but before he could say a word, she resumed her argument. Though her voice was quieter, it held no less conviction.

"There are other reasons why, if you had to have a child, I'd be a perfect mother for it. I'm smart—between you and me, the child wouldn't lack for brains. I'm patient, compassionate and even-tempered."

"You're also the head of a demanding corporation. How in the hell are you going to mother a child with all that work? Are you going to leave the poor kid with a nanny all day?"

Jenna was offended and let it show. "Not on your life. I'm not having a baby just to add it to my résumé. I'm having it because I want to mother it, and I can afford to do that precisely because I *am* the head of a demanding corporation. I have a support staff that's capable of handling the day-to-day running of things, and I already have an office set up at home with phones and a fax. If I want to work, I can do it while the baby naps, and if I don't want to work, I don't have to. For that matter, if I feel like setting up a crib at McCue's, I will. I'm the boss—I can do what I want. I don't plan to hire a nanny at all, because I won't be needing one. I'll hire sitters sometimes, because there may be important meetings I'll want to attend and also because I think it's healthy for me *and* the baby. But I'll be its primary caretaker. Me, and no one else."

Fixing her eyes on his, she offered what she felt was her most powerful point. "I'll make a great mother because I want this baby so much. I'm not a teenager riding on a whim. I'm a mature woman who has thought out every angle. I can afford to have this baby. I can afford to give it every advantage in the world. And I can handle single parenthood. It may not be easy, but nothing worthwhile ever is. The important thing is that I *want this baby.*"

He nudged her shoulder to get her moving back in the direction of the steps to the lawn, but the pace he set was a comfortable one. Jenna dared to hope that he was beginning to see the merits of the plan.

"I take it you discussed this with Caroline."

"I have no family, and she's my closest friend," Jenna said. "She's known for years that I wanted a baby. When I first started considering artificial insemination, I discussed it with her. Then, when it occurred to me that you would be an ideal donor, I bounced the idea off her. She agrees that it's good."

"She would. Do my parents know anything about it?"

"Oh, no. I won't say anything to them. It's not their decision to make. It's yours and mine." She looked up at him. His profile was strong, made more so by his brooding expression. "My arguments are good, Spencer. You know they are."

"They only go so far. They totally ignore several pertinent matters."

"Like what?" Jenna asked in surprise. She was sure she'd covered everything. For the past few months, she had thought of nothing but this.

"The moral considerations on my part. I'm not looking to have a child, but if I were to agree to help you out, there would be a child of mine, flesh of my flesh, alive in the world. It's fine and dandy for you to say that you don't want me around, but don't you think I'd wonder about the child? Don't you think I'd feel some kind of responsibility toward it?"

"I'm absolving you of responsibility. I'll have papers drawn up to that effect, if you'd like."

"You're missing the point. The point is *me*—" he jabbed his chest with the side of one loafer "—inside me. I'm not a block of wood. One of the reasons I don't want to have children is that I'm not a good candidate for fatherhood. My work takes me all over the world. I'm never in one place longer than several months at a stretch. I go where I want, when I want, and I like it that way. If I had kids, I'd feel guilty doing that."

"There'd be no need for guilt. The ground rules here would be different. You could do your part and then forget about it."

"Come off it, Jenna," he snapped, and quickened his pace. "What about illness? What if the child developed something? Don't you think I'd feel anything? What if, God forbid, it needed a transplant of some sort? Do you think I could ignore that? And then there's the practical matter of getting you pregnant in the first place! Your doctor may have a standard procedure for this, but, according to what you say, that standard procedure requires that I be here at the time you're ovulating. Correct?"

"Yes," she said, working to keep up with him.

"Well, what if I'm not? You want fresh sperm, but what if I'm halfway around the world."

"Florida isn't halfway around the world. You said you'd be in the Keys for a while."

He stopped and scowled at her. "Did you set me up for that? Did you deliberately get me to tell you that to strengthen your argument?"

"No, I—"

"Your argument isn't strengthened at all." He set off again. "I'd have to be here to donate *fresh* sperm at the very time you're ovulating, which means dropping everything I'm doing to sit in a little room and whistle a happy tune. And what happens if it doesn't take? What happens if you don't get pregnant the first time? Does your doctor's standard procedure guarantee results?"

"Of course not," Jenna said, climbing the steps to the lawn only slightly behind him. "It may take a while."

"A while? Two months, three, four?"

"Maybe."

"And I'm supposed to fly up here each time and do my little thing?"

"I'm asking you a favor, Spencer. A *favor*."

"Hey, you guys!" Caroline called, coming at them across the lawn at the same time that they cleared the steps. "We were beginning to think you drowned."

Spencer sputtered out a mocking sound, but he didn't push his sister away when she slipped an arm around his waist. That didn't mean she was fully escaping his wrath. Gruffly he said, "Did you honestly think I'd go for this, Caroline?"

Caroline shot a worried look at Jenna, who had come to a halt on her other side. "He's mad?"

"Not mad," Jenna murmured. "He just needs more convincing."

Rising instantly to the cause, Caroline told Spencer, "I think it's a wonderful idea. Mom and Dad aren't the only ones who want you to have a child. I do, too. I miss you when you're gone, and you're gone all the time. If I had a little Spencer to be an aunt to, I'd be in heaven.

If my best friend was my niece or nephew's mother, I'd be in *seventh* heaven."

"Yeah, and you think our parents would leave it at that? They'd be *demanding* that I marry Jenna and give the baby our name."

"That's out of the question," Jenna said with such force that both pairs of Smith eyes flew to hers. She looked straight at Spencer. "From the start, I told you I didn't want to get married, and I mean it. I'm not looking for a husband—I'm not looking for in-laws— I'm not looking for an aunt or grandparents for my child. I'm not looking for money, and I'm not looking for a name. My baby will be a McCue. So, much as I love them, if your parents start pushing for marriage, I'll fight them even harder than you will."

"You will?" Caroline asked with blatant disappointment.

"I *told* you I would, Caroline. From the very beginning, from the very first time I mentioned this to you, that was one of the ground rules. I don't—want—to get—married. *All* I *want* is a *baby*."

"Which brings us back to the point I was trying to make," Spencer said. "What if you don't conceive right away? I can't be running back here month after month to fill little jars with—"

Caroline interrupted. "Uh, I think I hear Annie calling." Dropping away from Spencer, she leaned close to Jenna. "Love your hair ribbon. It looks slightly Milan. An Armani derivative, maybe?" With a wink, she was off.

Jenna gently released the necktie and handed it back to Spencer. "The wind isn't bad up here. Thanks."

"You should have left it on. It looked risqué. But then—" his eyes touched hers "—you're not the risqué type. You're straight-laced and conservative and proper. I can't believe you're thinking of having a child out of wedlock."

"What an outdated expression."

"It describes what you're doing."

"Lots of women are doing it."

"Women in prominent positions like yours?"

"Some."

"It's very daring."

She didn't blink. "Okay, so I'm daring."

"I wouldn't have thought that of you."

"Most people wouldn't, but I really don't care. I want a child. I'm willing to be daring to get it. Will you help?"

He grimaced. "Hell, Jenna, you don't know what you're asking."

"I do. I—"

She was interrupted by Spencer's father, who hailed them as he crossed the lawn toward his son. "Come see the Watsons, Spence. They've been asking for you all afternoon, and they have to leave soon." He threw an arm around Spencer's shoulder, which was level with his. Spencer had clearly inherited his blue eyes from his father, but Joe's blue, like his hair, had paled with age. "They weren't here the last time you were home, and they may not be here the next. How 'bout it?"

"Sure," Spencer said.

Jenna shot him a look that said "Coward."

He regarded her with deliberate poise. "Want to come see the Watsons with me?"

Jenna had seen the Watsons earlier, which was more than enough for her. They were well advanced in age and profoundly hard of hearing. Conversations with them were exercises in futility. The most one could do was to smile, nod or laugh in response to whatever they chose to say, and since most of what they chose to say was based on their warped perception of what the rest of the world had to say, the encounter was often painful. Jenna could just imagine their seeing her with Spencer and drawing the kind of conclusion that she didn't want. Worse, she could imagine them airing that conclusion in the loud voices for which they were known.

"Thanks," she said with a sweet smile, "but I think I'll go comb my hair. It's a mess."

"Join us when you're done," the elder Smith invited. "You look good beside Spence."

Dying a little inside, Jenna turned away, but not fast enough to miss the scowl Spencer sent her. She hadn't taken more than two steps before she realized he still had her shoes. When she turned back, he was taking them from his pockets. He separated himself from his father long enough to return them.

"He smells something," he muttered.

"Not from me."

"Did Caroline talk?"

"She promised she wouldn't."

"If he starts pushing, I'm outta here."

"If he starts pushing, tell him to mind his own business."

Spencer snorted, shoved the shoes into her hands and turned back to his father. Without further ado, Jenna went on toward the house, but it wasn't until she was upstairs, leaning back against the door in the privacy of the bathroom adjoining Caroline's childhood bedroom, that she put a hand to her heart, closed her eyes and wondered where she stood.

He hadn't said yes.

He hadn't said no.

She slipped the hand to her belly, where it rested ever so lightly. Oh, how she wanted a baby. The longing was an ache deep inside, a tingle of anticipation, a shimmer of excitement. She pictured her womb, pictured an embryo forming in the vaguest of human shapes, pictured that embryo evolving into a fetus. Her breasts seemed to swell at the thought, then her heart when she imagined that fetus becoming a ready-to-be-born child.

If she had to, she would use the sperm bank. But the warmth inside her took on a special glow when she thought of her child being Spencer's.

3

AT TWO IN THE MORNING, Jenna's phone rang. Though she hadn't been sleeping, the sound was jarring in the stillness of night. Her heart pounded as she reached across the magazines that lay beside her in bed and picked up the receiver.

"Hello?"

"Did I wake you?"

The low voice was male and distinctive, and did nothing to calm her pulse. She pressed a hand to her breast. "No. I was reading." After the briefest of hesitations, she asked, "Where are you?"

"In Newport. At the house."

Jenna was in her own house, across the Seekonk River from him in Little Compton. "We all assumed you'd flown back to Florida." That would have been a typically Spencer thing to do. "I waited in Newport on the slim chance that you hadn't and would come back and talk with me. When everyone else went to bed, I ran out of an excuse to stay." She hadn't wanted to give the elder Smiths the slightest cause for speculation about something going on between Spencer and her.

"I was visiting a friend," he said. "I hadn't seen him for years. Someone at the party told me he'd been sick. We've been talking all this time."

"You don't have to explain."

"No, but I want to. I'm not heartless. I could see that what you asked me this afternoon means a lot to you.

I wouldn't have left without giving you some kind of answer."

Jenna held her breath.

"The problem," he went on, "is that I don't have enough information to give you any kind of answer."

Her hopes rose. "Then you're considering it?"

"Not seriously. I still think the whole thing's absurd."

She thought back over the years to some of the stories that had filtered back to Rhode Island from wherever Spencer was. "You do absurd things all the time."

"I do *daring* things all the time," he corrected, "and I only do them after I've researched them inside and out."

He hadn't said no. *He hadn't said no.* "I've researched this inside and out," she told him. "Ask me anything. Go ahead. I'll tell you whatever you want to know."

"I want to know more about you and why you want to do this."

"I want a baby. It's as simple as that."

"But *why* do you want a baby?"

Jenna didn't know what to say. She thought the answer was obvious.

Spencer must have taken her silence as criticism of the question, because he said, "I have a right to know. After all, you're suggesting that you be the mother of my child, and you're saying you'd be its primary caretaker. So whereas donating my sperm would be the beginning and end of my role in this endeavor, yours would be more far-reaching. If being a mother has become an obsession with you, the child will suffer. I wouldn't want to be party to the creation of a child that would be raised by an obsessive woman."

"I'm not obsessive. I've never been obsessive." Strong-willed, perhaps. Stubborn or determined or dedicated. But never obsessive.

"Then tell me why you want this baby."

She pushed up against the headboard, shifting to get the pillows more comfortably arranged. She pulled the white comforter to her waist, grasped the white sheet a bit higher. She settled the phone more securely against her ear.

"Well?" he prodded.

"I'm organizing my thoughts. I've wanted a baby for so long, and there are so many reasons why. Are you comfortable? This could take a while."

"The organizing?"

"The telling."

"I'm comfortable."

"Are you in the den?" She pictured the room. It was on the ground floor of the Smiths' house and was paneled in mahogany. Large, heavy-handed oils hung on the walls between books and electronic gadgets. It was a dark room, a man's room. She could see Spencer there.

"I'm in my bedroom."

That was a different story. She had more trouble picturing him there. The room was exactly as it had been when he had graduated from college, with banners on the walls and trophies on the shelves. It was a boy's room, but Spencer had left boyhood far behind. He was forty-one, with a harsh scar to attest to the dangers he'd met and a mature and imposing body to match.

"No comment?" he asked.

"No."

"Want to know what I'm wearing?"

"No."

"That's good, because I'd be hard put to come up with a respectable answer."

He was testing her, she knew. He was trying to see if she was squeamish, which would matter if she had a son. "You're not wearing anything?" she asked nonchalantly. "Aren't you cold?" Her cheeks weren't. Thought of Spencer sprawled naked on his bed heated them, and the thought wouldn't seem to fade.

"Are *you* cold?" he asked in a low, silky voice.

"I'm wearing clothes."

"At two in the morning?"

"A nightgown. I'm always cold."

"You need a man to warm you."

The statement was a sexist one. She might have taken offense if she hadn't been so sure of her feelings. "I have a goose-down comforter. I pull it up when I'm cold and throw it aside when I'm not. I drop my dry cleaning on it and pile my books on it, and I've been known to stamp around on it when I'm cleaning the dust off the ceiling fan. It takes whatever abuse I heap on it, and it doesn't complain. It's more indulgent and less demanding than any man would be."

Spencer was quiet for a minute. When he spoke again, his tone was serious. "A baby might throw up all over your comforter. It might keep you up all night if it had a fever, make you sit in the doctor's office for hours the next day. It might cry every time you tried to put it back in its crib. How would you feel then?"

"Badly, if the baby was sick. Helpless, if there was nothing to do but wait out the bug. Certainly more than willing to hold the poor thing if that was the only relief it could get."

"But why do you want that?" he asked, returning to his original question. "You have a perfectly orderly life.

A baby will destroy orderly in a few short days, and it won't be restored for eighteen long years. Have you thought of that?"

"I have."

"And you're still game?"

"I am."

"*Why?*"

He sounded as though he was without a clue, legitimately puzzled about why she would willingly and knowingly wreak havoc with her life. He was challenging her, demanding that she make her case in a way that he could understand. She sensed that he was also looking for reasons why he should father a child.

After only the shortest pause this time, she said, "I guess the best way to explain it is to go chronologically." Her gaze touched the scrolled picture frame on the dresser. The faces smiling from it made her heart catch. "It's been eight years since my parents' plane went down. I was twenty-seven when that happened, and over the next three years, I was too busy dealing with the immediate future to think of the distant one. Then I turned thirty. McCue's was healthy. I was relaxed at its helm. I had time to think about my parents' deaths and my own mortality, and it hit me that the McCue name would die with me." As fate had it, she came from generations of single-child families. "I'm the last one left. If I die, McCue's will be sold. There's no one to pass it to. That's sad."

"You could have a child who doesn't want a thing to do with McCue's."

"True, but at least that child would have the proceeds from it to hopefully do something worthwhile with his or her life, and the thought of that gives me comfort. I don't want my family line to end with me."

After a moment, he said, "Okay. I can buy that. For starters."

"And that's all it was. Once I had the bug in my ear, I couldn't get it out. At first, it was just that idea of keeping the family line going, but then the physical part began."

Her hair was in a ponytail high enough on her head to be out of the way when she slept. She wrapped her fingers around the band and drew them the length of dark waves to the ponytail's end. It was a gesture she had made hundreds of times in her life, usually when she was either deep in thought or nervous. She was a little of each just then.

"I'm listening," Spencer said.

Her voice was softer. "I know. It's harder to explain this part."

"Take your time."

What she took was a deep breath. Time wouldn't help, not when she had always been self-conscious about intimate things, and certainly not when she kept thinking of him lying buck naked in bed. So she spit out the words with begrudging resignation. "I became aware of my body. I was made a certain way for certain reasons, and I wasn't fulfilling those reasons."

"What do you mean?" he asked.

He was a virile man with a knowledge of sex that she couldn't begin to match. She assumed he was being purposely dense. "You know what I mean."

"I want you to explain."

She closed her eyes. When she opened them, she focused on the driftwood sculpture she had bought in the Bahamas several years before. It reminded her of sun and sand, and was totally asexual. It took her mind off Spencer. "I have ovaries to create a child with, a uterus to carry a child in and breasts to put a child to. I haven't done any of those things. It's a waste, wouldn't you say?"

"That depends on what else you do with those things. Children aren't the only beneficiaries of breasts and ovaries. Men can be, too."

She forgot about the driftwood sculpture as a tingle ran up her spine. She shifted her hip against the sheet and laid her hand lightly between her breasts. "Ovaries?" she asked weakly. "How do men benefit from ovaries?"

"Ovaries produce the hormones that make you different from me. They affect the way you look, the way you smell, the way you respond to me."

She wasn't touching any of that. Thin ice wasn't something she skated on for long. She took a shaky breath. "Okay. Well. I was talking about my body in relation to having children, and when it comes to that, I'm feeling very unfulfilled."

"Clearly you're unfulfilled when it comes to men, too."

"Why do you say that?" she asked in a huff.

"Because you're all but dragging men off the street in a bid for sperm."

She sat up straight. "I am *not* dragging men off the street. You are the only man I've asked; and I did that for specific reasons. Just because I don't know any other men whose genes I'd want doesn't mean I'm not *involved* with any men."

"Are you?"

"That's none of your business!"

"Oh, but it is," he said smoothly. "There are health issues involved, for one thing. You've told me you don't want a man around the house, but if you're hopping from one bachelor pad to another when you get the urge for sex, you could have picked up a disease. Me, I was using condoms long before it became the rage, because I didn't want to risk any unplanned pregnancies, but other guys may not be so careful."

"I don't have any diseases. I'm healthy. I told you that."

"Okay, then there's the issue of having men around this child you're proposing to have. I wouldn't like the idea of a child of mine having a stream of 'uncles' coming in and out of its life, any more than I'd like the idea of your leaving the kid with a sitter and running out for sex four or five nights a week. So are you sexually involved with any men at this time or not?"

"Not," she said, because the issue of pride was nothing compared to the issue of having a child. If letting Spencer Smith know that her social life was lousy was a condition of his donating his sperm, she'd do it.

"When was the last time you were sexually involved with someone?"

She swallowed. "Three years ago."

"Who was he?"

"A journalist from New York. I met him at a show in Paris. We were together there, then briefly when we got back."

"And before him?"

She plucked at the sheet. "There was an accountant a few years before that."

"A few?" he prodded.

"Four. We were together a month." She pushed herself on, but angrily and feeling suddenly close to tears. Remembering past relationships made her feel empty. "Before him, there was a guy I met in business school, and that's it. Not exactly a history of wildness. Nothing resembling nymphomania. Nothing to corrupt a child with. If I picked up a disease, it would have already shown up. You can call my doctor, if you'd like. He'll testify that I'm clean." She pressed a hand to her upper lip and held it there until the lip had stopped quivering. The effort preoccupied her, so much so that she didn't realize how quiet Spencer was until he finally spoke.

"That won't be necessary. I trust you."

"Well, thank goodness for that."

"But I had a right to ask."

It had hurt to list failed relationships that way, but he did have a point. She had put some of the very same questions to Caroline, who knew as much about Spencer's love life as anyone did. Spencer's comment about condoms confirmed what Caroline had already told her.

"So—" his voice came over the line more gently "— you want a baby, first, to carry on the McCue name, and second, to fulfill the maternal functions of your body. Is that it?"

"No, that's not *it*. I haven't mentioned the most important part." But she didn't immediately go on. She needed a minute to gather herself, to put the past aside and focus on the future, to ease the gruffness from her voice and be her well-balanced self.

When she remained silent, he asked softly, "Are you falling asleep on me?"

Fat chance, she thought. "No. I'm organizing again. The next part has to do with emotions. It's the most important part. But I'm not sure where to begin."

"Begin anywhere. I'll sort things out when you're done."

She took a breath and, letting the rigidity out of her spine, slid her hand palm up into her lap. Taking him at his word, she began to toss out her thoughts. "I want to hold a baby and not have to give it back at the end of the day. I want to take care of a baby, to know what it likes to eat and how it likes to eat and what each little cry means. I want to love a baby and be loved back. I've watched Caroline raise her children—" she warmed at the image that came to mind "—and there's something heart-stopping when they're small and they throw their little arms around your neck and hold on for dear life. I want that."

"They don't stay small for long," Spencer pointed out.

"I know, and I know the saying that the bigger they get, the bigger their problems, but I can handle the problems. It's the love that's important. The outward demonstration of that love changes as they grow—it certainly did with my parents and me—but the love is always there. I want that." She rushed on. "I want noise in this house and toys on these floors. I want a direction to my life beyond business. I want someone to buy clothes for and take to the movies and go to Disneyland with. I want someone to think about besides myself. I want someone to worry about." She caught her breath and deliberately slowed. "That may sound obsessive to you, but, believe me, it isn't. Through it all, I'll still be a businesswoman. I love my work. I can make it take more or less of my time, but I won't ever let it go completely, and that means I won't be hung up when my child goes off to first grade or, even more, to college. I'll always have the business to keep things in balance."

She was silent a moment before continuing. "But the business alone isn't enough. It was when my parents first died, when I was overwhelmed trying to take things over and keep things growing. Then things settled down, and little by little I saw the hole in my life. I want a child to help fill it, a child of my own, someone with a blood bond. I want that *connection*. I don't have it with anyone else in the world." She curled her hand into a fist. Her voice was suddenly smaller, diminished by the overwhelming yearning she was trying to describe. "There are times . . ." She paused.

"Times what?"

"Times when I feel so *lonely* for family. Times when..." She struggled with the emotion, and he didn't rush her. "Times when I feel like I have so much feeling inside me with no place to put it. Times when I feel like I'll *burst*." She paused again, then sighed. "Does this mean anything to you?"

He didn't answer.

"It probably doesn't. You have a family. You have grandparents, parents, aunts, uncles and cousins, a sister, two nephews and a niece. Whenever you want you can come home to people you love and who love you. Do you know how precious that is, Spencer?"

He remained silent.

"Oh, look," she went on apologetically, "I'm not saying you don't, and I'm certainly not criticizing you. You've chosen to be footloose and fancy free, and that's your right. You like your life. It's exciting and busy and full. You don't suffer from attacks of the lonelies. I'm not sure many men do. They're more self-contained than we are. They don't crave the soft, warm, silly family things women do." She leaned back against the pillows. "If I'd been born a man, my life would be perfect."

"I'm glad you weren't born a man" came the deep voice from the other end of the line just as Jenna was beginning to think *he'd* fallen asleep. "You're too pretty for that."

She didn't know what to say. Spencer had never given her a compliment before. She had always been his younger sister's best friend, and not even with Caroline was he a compliment giver. His affection for her came out in his interest in the things she was doing and in her children. Jenna had been simply one of the things Caroline was doing.

The compliment was kind, though Jenna didn't delude herself into thinking that he meant anything deep by it. No doubt, since she had just painted a picture of how alone she was in the world, he was feeling sorry for her.

Feeling strangely awkward and doubly grateful that they were talking on the phone rather than in person, she said in a quiet voice, "Well, that's neither here nor there. Have you decided whether I'd be a good mother for your child?"

"If I wanted a child, you'd be fine."

She sat straight again. "Then you'll do it?"

"I don't know if I want a child. I told you that this afternoon. I need time to decide."

"But I wanted to start on this soon."

"How soon?"

"I'll be ovulating in two weeks. You said you'd give me an answer before you leave."

"I will. That gives me another twelve hours to make a decision."

"Is it so difficult, Spencer?" she pleaded. "A few minutes of your time this month, maybe next. I won't ask a thing of you after that. Not a thing, and you'll have that in writing."

"I wasn't planning to have a child."

"But this will be like *not* having one, only your parents will be pleased."

He snorted. "Yeah, and they'll start in on me about coming home for the kid's birthday and Christmas, and they'll nag—"

"They won't," Jenna interrupted. She had strong feelings about that. "If you agree to this, and if I do get pregnant, I'll tell them the truth. They'll know that you were doing a favor to me, that I've insisted that your role be limited to the child's conception, and that I have sole custody. I've talked this part out with Caroline. She agrees that given the choice between accepting my rules or alienating themselves from my child, they'll let you be."

"But I don't *need* a child."

"I *do*."

Seconds stretched into minutes. When Jenna couldn't bear the thudding of her heart any longer, she said, "Spencer? Will you?"

"You have guts," he declared in a way that said he thought she was either very brave or very crazy. "I don't think there's another woman on this earth who'd ask me to do what you have."

"I'm desperate. I want my baby to be the absolute very best. For that, I need the absolute very best man, and you're the absolute very best man."

"Oh, please."

"It's the truth. Will you do it?"

"I don't want to."

"I know, but you're considering it." She held her breath.

He swore under his. She could picture him plowing a hand through his hair much as he'd done on the dock that afternoon. "Look," he said with a long-suffering sigh, "the best I can offer to do is to give it more thought. Can we meet later?"

"Name the time and place, and I'll be there."

After a minute, he grumbled, "Hell, I don't know when or where. I'll call you tomorrow. Will you be around?"

"All day. I won't go anywhere. I'll wait for your call. Spencer, thanks. I really appreciate your doing this."

"I haven't said I'd do anything."

"But you haven't said no. You're thinking about it, and that's all I can ask. If you decide you can't, I'll be really disappointed, but I'll understand. It wouldn't be right for you to feel forced into doing something that you're against either for moral reasons or for reasons that—"

"Go to bed, Jenna," he cut in. "I can't think when you babble. I'll call you later. 'Bye."

4

SPENCER COULD HAVE easily killed Caroline. Lying in bed, feeling distinctly disgruntled at three in the morning, he swore he would have, if he didn't love her so much. But she had always held a special place in his heart. From infancy, she had adored him. Sure, his parents had loved him, but not in the unconditional way Caroline had, and in turn, he had used his six-year edge to protect her whenever he could. Time had put physical distance between them, as had the needs of their individual personalities. As she'd grown older, Caroline had even had a thing or two to say about his nomadic life-style. Still, she indulged him more than his parents did. She made Newport a less confining place for him.

Usually.

But she'd done it this time. She had actually told Jenna that he might go along with the idea of donating sperm for Jenna's cause, and though no one had told him he had to do it, though no one was holding a gun to his head or binding his arms and legs and milking his seed from him, he felt trapped in an invisible—and infuriating—kind of way.

Jenna was sweet and sincere. She was pretty in a dark-eyed, dark-haired, creamy skinned, well-bred kind of way. In the same well-bred kind of way, she was a successful businesswoman. He was sure she would make a good mother. He was also sure that despite any protestation she might make, she had her heart set on his helping her, which meant she would be crushed if he refused.

But he didn't want to have a child. He didn't want the responsibility—and he meant what he'd told Jenna: he would be aware of that responsibility no matter how fervently she absolved him of it. He didn't want to know that a child of his was alive in the world while he was running around having fun. True, it wasn't an irresponsible kind of fun. It was self-supporting, even profitable when he tallied in the proceeds from sales of his books and movie rights. Still, it was fun.

If only Caroline had nixed the idea from the start. If only she had told Jenna that he wouldn't go for it or that he would be furious if she asked, he wouldn't be in such a mess. But Jenna had asked him, and she'd done it in a way that had made it very, very difficult for him to turn her down—because some of her points were valid. He didn't want them to be. He wanted the idea of single motherhood to be totally off the wall, but it wasn't, at least not as Jenna proposed it. She had thought everything out. She had the means, the desire and, he was sure, the natural aptitude for motherhood. She was also right about his parents being thrilled and, therefore, appeased where his leaving an heir was concerned—which raised another point that she had made that kept sticking in his mind. His estate was as sizable as Jenna's, but he didn't have a direct heir for it, either. Not to mention the fact that they *would* make a good baby together, he and Jenna. She was right there, too.

So. What was he supposed to do? She was offering him something that he hadn't considered before but that had some merits. If he turned her down, he might never get another offer like it. If he turned her down, he might be sorry in ten or twenty years. If, God forbid, something happened to one or both of his parents the way it had happened to Jenna's, would he be sorry he hadn't given them the gift of a grandchild? If something happened to *him*, would he lie on his deathbed wishing he was leaving behind something more of his body than a golden urn filled with ashes?

He swore loudly and turned away from the light of the moon. Sweet, innocent Jenna had opened a can of worms. He kept trying to close it, kept trying to simply make the decision to see her in the morning and tell her no, then fly back to Florida and immerse himself in his work, but he couldn't make that decision. Something was holding him back. Some gut instinct.

Spencer had been in many a precarious position in the course of his travels, and if there was one thing he knew, it was that his gut instinct was sound, damn it.

JENNA HAD TROUBLE falling asleep. She didn't know whether to be hopeful or discouraged by Spencer's call. She hadn't realized how much she'd set her heart on using his sperm, until she realized that within hours she might know that she couldn't. Then again, if he said yes, she'd be on her way to having the most incredible child in the world. The excitement of that thought alone kept her up for a while.

She fell asleep shortly before dawn, which was probably why she didn't hear the doorbell when it first rang. She didn't rouse until the tone was coming in imperious bursts of threes, and then it was a minute before she could correctly identify the sound. She stumbled from bed and was at the bedroom door before she thought of covering herself. Ducking back in to snatch the decorative throw from the back of the wicker chair, she wrapped it around her and ran barefoot down the stairs.

Squinting out the sidelight, she felt a moment's panic. Spencer was standing there, looking freshly showered and awake enough to make her acutely aware of how awful she appeared. Her hair was a mess; her eyes were still only half opened; she was sure there were pillowcase creases on her face.

But he had seen her peering out, so she couldn't pretend she wasn't home. And anyway, she wouldn't do that. If he had made a decision, she wanted to know what it was.

Clutching the throw around her with one hand, she opened the door with the other. The sun hit her full face. She swayed sideways to use his large frame as a shade.

"What time is it?" she asked in a sleep-gritty voice.

"Eight-forty," he answered, sounding remorseless as he took in her disheveled appearance.

Wondering how he could look so good with so little sleep, Jenna swallowed and pushed loose wisps of hair back from her face. "Want to come in? It'll take me just a minute to put something on."

"Don't dress on my behalf," he said.

She took that to mean he wouldn't be staying long enough to make it worth her bother, and felt an immediate stab of disappointment. "You won't do it?" Tears sprang to her eyes. "Oh, Spencer—"

"I didn't say I wouldn't." He scowled at the tears. "There are a few more things I need to know."

"Oh. Okay." She glanced around, not sure whether to lead him into the living room or the kitchen. She wished she could think clearly, but his appearance had caught her off guard at a time of day when she was at her worst. "Uh, let me make coffee." The making would buy her time; the drinking would help clear her head.

Maintaining a grip on the throw, she went into the kitchen. Though she sensed Spencer behind her, she didn't look around. Rather, she did the best she could putting on a pot of coffee to brew. Working one-handed slowed her, but she didn't dare let go of the throw for fear it would fall to the floor. Her nightgown was of fine, soft, translucent cotton. She had nothing on underneath.

The instant she had the coffee machine gurgling, she said, "I'm running upstairs. I'll be back down in a second."

"Sit," Spencer ordered.

"But I'm not dressed," she protested, daring to look at him. It was a mistake. His scar was like an exclamation mark after his order, and above that, his eyes were compellingly blue. Though they didn't move from her face, she felt their touch all over.

"What we're discussing is pretty intimate," he said. "You're dressed just fine."

She wanted to argue but was loath to anger him. So she slipped into a chair at the small glass table and sat looking as poised as possible with the throw protecting her virtue, her legs pressed together and her ankles crossed and tucked under the chair.

Spencer leaned against the counter. He was wearing slim-fitting black pants and a loose black shirt. His hair had been parted and combed to the side, but spikes were already falling over his brow. In keeping with the scar, they gave him a commanding look, which he accentuated by folding his arms across his chest.

He regarded her steadily. "You mentioned basal body temperature. Explain that term."

She refused to squirm. "That's what my temperature is when my body is at total rest. I take my temperature every morning when I first wake up, even before I sit up in bed. Then I record it on a chart."

"You've already been doing that?"

"For three months, every morning. Except this one," she added, since it was obvious that she hadn't taken time for anything when the doorbell had rung. "But that's okay. I can miss a day or two. I know what my temperature would have been if I'd taken it."

"How?"

"There's a distinct pattern." More quietly she added, "And I'm very regular."

As though mocking her shyness, he said in a bold voice, "This relates to your period, I take it."

"Yes."

He waited, then gestured for her to continue. "Come on. Tell me. I want to know how it works."

The fact that he was listening and considering her request lifted her spirits above the self-consciousness she felt. "My temperature is below normal on the days leading up to ovulation. It usually drops even more when I actually ovulate, then starts to rise after that. It keeps going up until I get my period."

"So the exact day of ovulation is the critical one?"

"Kind of."

"What do you mean, kind of?"

"According to my doctor, it's best if sperm is already in the fallopian tube when I ovulate, which means doing his procedure just prior to that time. Actually," she mustered the courage to say, "if you were willing to hang around for a few days, he'd do the procedure twice."

"Twice, huh?" Spencer said.

"Only if you were willing," she rushed on. "I've done so much reading on this, and the books seem to agree that when a couple is trying to conceive, they should have intercourse, ideally, every other day around the time of ovulation. That gives the sperm count time to fully recover, and since sperm will stay alive for forty-eight to seventy-two hours, every other day makes sense—but that's for *couples,* and we're not a couple in *that* sense. I know you have other things to do, and that you don't like being around here with your parents and all, so if you could do it once, that'd be great. I mean, it could be that I'll conceive—" she snapped her fingers "—like that."

"It could be," he drawled, "that we'd need to do it a whole *lot* of times before you conceive." The look in his eye grew speculative. He dropped his gaze to her neck, which was encased in lace, then her breasts, which were bound by the throw, then her belly, which rested somewhere under multiple folds of fabric.

Jenna wanted to hide. She felt naked and exposed, and decidedly inferior to every other woman Spencer had been involved with. True, what she was proposing didn't mean *that* kind of involvement, but he was right. It would be a pretty intimate thing if she carried his child.

"I'll do it," he said.

Her heart tripped. "You will?"

He nodded.

She came to her feet with a huge smile. "You will?" She brought her hands together in front of that smile and looked at him through tears of happiness this time.

He made a sound that told her what she thought of the tears. Then he said, "On one condition."

"I'll do whatever you want." She beamed, feeling lighter and brighter than she had in weeks. "I'm so grateful, Spencer, *so* grateful, and relieved! I thought for sure you'd say no and then I'd have to use the sperm bank, and this way my baby will be perfect, absolutely perfect!"

"No artificial insemination."

Her breath caught. The smile faded. "No what?"

"Artificial insemination," he repeated. "It's the real thing or nothing."

"The real thing?" she asked.

He looked as if he wanted to grin but was holding it back. "Sexual intercourse, between you and me."

Jenna felt suddenly weak in the knees. Dropping back into the chair, she clutched the throw to her chest. "We can't do that," she said in dismay. "We're not like that with each other."

"We can be if you want my baby."

"I do, I do." She made a helpless face. "But you don't know what you're saying!"

"I know exactly what I'm saying. I've been thinking about it all night. I'm saying that if you're going to have my baby, I want it conceived the normal way. I'm also saying that I won't stand in a little room and pleasure myself when you could do that for me."

"But you're Caroline's brother!"

"So?"

"So, I'm like a sister to you."

Very slowly he shook his head.

"But I'm not good at sex!" she protested. As mortifying as it was, she had to tell him the truth. "I've been with three men, and none of them raved about my skill. I don't think I could *begin* to pleasure you."

"You could begin," he assured her, and his voice was suddenly thicker, "and I'd show you what to do from there."

"But you've been with so many women! You're so experienced! You're so *big!*" She grasped on to that. "You said it yourself—I'm too short. You're nearly a foot taller than me."

"You liked that when you were thinking of having a boy."

"I *do* like it, but that was when I thought we'd be doing this in a doctor's office. Honestly, Spencer, it would be so much better that way."

"Maybe for you. Not for me. And since I'm the one this thing hangs on..." Unfolding his arms, he straightened away from the counter. "Need time to think, Jenna? I'll give you time." He strolled toward the door. "Take as much time as you want. I'll be in Florida for the next six months, but after that I could be God knows where. Caroline has the number of my place in the Keys. You could leave a message, then when I get back—"

"Wait," she cried just as his foot cleared the threshold. She couldn't let him walk away, not when she was so close to getting what she wanted. "Okay." She rose from the chair, determined to commit herself before she could be paralyzed by shyness. "Okay, we'll do it that way if you want." She could handle it; she knew she could. "We'll do it that way."

A small smile lifted one side of his mouth. "Good."

"But will you promise me one thing in return?" she begged. "If it doesn't work that way—I mean, if you can't—if I can't help you—" She sucked in a breath and pushed it out with the words "If the actual act is a total disaster, will you do it my way?" Her cheeks burned, but she held steady.

"The act won't be a disaster."

"Don't be so sure. I'm *really* not good at this."

He frowned. "You think you won't turn me on?" He started toward her.

"It's been known to happen."

"I find that hard to believe."

"It happened."

He stood directly before her. "With all three of your lovers?"

"With the last."

"Then that was his problem. It won't be mine."

"How do you know? Here we stand, fully dressed— at least, you are, and I'm covered up. How do you know what will happen when we're in bed? This is like a business arrangement, for goodness' sake. Is it realistic to expect that you'll be turned on enough to—" she swallowed "—enough to . . ."

"Come?"

She nodded.

"Yes, it's realistic to expect that," he said. Lifting a hand, he ran the backs of his fingers along the side of her breast.

Jenna gasped in surprise. Her first instinct was to move away, but the lightness of his touch and the fact of who he was and what she had asked of him, held her to him. Within seconds, she'd begun to tremble inside. Eyes riveted to his dark face, she saw the small, seeming involuntary rise of his head and the faint flare of his nostrils. There was nothing more by way of touching, just the backs of his fingers shaping her breast through two layers of fabric for what couldn't have been more than another ten seconds, before he dropped his hand to her waist, then away. In the next instant he looked down at himself. Jenna followed his gaze to the swell of arousal at his fly.

"I don't think I'll have a problem," he remarked dryly.

Ridiculous, given the circumstances, but she felt guilty, as though she had walked in on him when he'd been performing a private act that had nothing to do with her. Unable to meet his eyes, she backed down into the chair.

"Anything else you want to test now?" he asked.

She studied her hands. "No."

"Want to change your mind about me fathering your child?"

She looked up at him. "No!"

He chuckled, then shot a glance at the coffee maker. "That smells good. I could use a cup. Want one?"

"Uh, sure," she said, but she didn't move. She let Spencer do the pouring, while she struggled to regain her poise. One part of her was near to bursting with excitement about the baby she was going to have. The other part was totally unsettled by the thought of what she was going to have to do to get it.

She took the cup and saucer he handed her and quickly put them down on the table so that the shaking of her hands wouldn't show, then she waited while he set down his own cup and took a seat across from her.

"Okay," he said, stretching out his legs, "let's talk specifics. Yesterday you said you'd be ovulating in two weeks. Do you have your period now?"

She focused on the coffee. "I'll be getting it tomorrow."

"How can you be sure?"

"I have a twenty-eight-day cycle. Always. Besides, I can feel it."

"You're crampy?"

"Bloated."

"You don't look bloated," he said, then tacked on, "not that I can see much more than your face, but that looks fine."

Jenna didn't believe him for a minute. She had barely had four hours' sleep, and she hadn't washed, hadn't combed her hair, hadn't put on a bit of makeup. As if that wasn't bad enough, she felt totally unprepared for the conversation they were having. She knew everything there was to know on the topic of artificial insemination, but Spencer had shifted topics on her. It wasn't fair.

She looked down at her coffee again. "Spencer?"

"Yes, Jenna?"

She heard his amusement and felt worse. "I'm very nervous about this."

"I can see that," he said gently. "But I thought I put your worries to rest."

"There's something else. It's the awkwardness. You're Caroline's brother. I never intended we'd actually have sex."

"Neither did I, but I spent all last night thinking about it, and I was hard then, too."

"You're just saying that."

"I'm not."

"You never would have thought of it if I hadn't drafted you."

"Maybe not," he admitted, "but only because I'm not around here enough to get ideas like that. Which raises another point. Where should we do it? The doctor's office is out."

She eyed him beseechingly. "You could reconsider. It'd be so much more controlled if we did it my way." She watched him take a drink of his coffee and set down his cup, and noticed that his hand didn't shake in the least. He looked as though he was enjoying the discussion. No self-consciousness on *his* part.

"I don't like things controlled," he said, "not things to do with sex. So. Where'll it be? My place or yours? We could use a hotel, but that'd be kind of sterile, don't you think?"

"Sterile is fine. After all, this is a business arrangement. It's not like it has to be romantic or anything. We'll only be doing it once."

"I thought you said the ideal thing was to do it every other day around the time you ovulate."

"We don't have to."

"If we're going to do this, we'll do it right. So. We should get together twelve days from now?"

Her stomach was jumping. *The baby. Think of the baby,* she told herself. "Twelve days. That sounds right."

"Unless you want to take a few months to get used to the idea."

Jenna didn't think *any* amount of time would get her used to the idea of having sex with Spencer. Figuring that she was best to get it over with, she gave a quick headshake. "I want to get pregnant as soon as possible. I'll be ovulating around the eighth of July, which means that if I conceive right away, the baby will be born next April."

"Boy, you've got that down pat."

"I've had plenty of time to count."

He finished off his coffee. "Then I should fly back here on the sixth?"

"If you could." She thought ahead to that time. "I had everything figured out when I assumed we'd be using artificial insemination. We would have been able to see the doctor separately during the day and go our own ways at night without even bumping into each other. I thought it would be less awkward that way." She grimaced. "This way will be more complicated."

"How so?" Spencer asked. He sank down in the chair, stretching his legs out even farther. "I don't see any complications. I'll stay here. You have plenty of room."

"*Here?*"

"My parents and I don't do well under the same roof. I doubt I'll even tell them I'm in town."

"But they'll want to see you."

"They won't miss me if they don't know I'm here."

"What if they see you around town?"

"They won't. I'll stay here the whole time."

Jenna had visions of trying to entertain him and proving as inept at that as she would be at sex. He was a man of action. He was used to exciting things happening, which they certainly wouldn't do in her stately old house. "Good Lord, Spencer, you'll be bored. Besides, I was planning to work."

"No sweat. You can work. You won't even have to break up your day to keep a doctor's appointment, since we'll be doing our thing at night."

At night. Of course. She supposed it would be easier in the dark. Then again, she doubted it would. Thought of being naked with Spencer—with Spencer Smith of the dashing scar, author, adventurer and expert on women—was daunting.

But she wanted that baby.

"We can't sleep together," she informed him in an attempt to set some rules that would make her less shaky. "I mean, we can't spend the whole night together."

He frowned. "Why not?"

"Because this is a business arrangement. It wouldn't be right."

He looked displeased. "But I was looking forward to having a warm body next to me. And what if we want to do it more than once? Am I supposed to run back and forth down the hall?"

"We can't do it more than once in one night. The books say that would be counterproductive. You'd be continually depleted."

Spencer arched a brow. "*Some* men might be depleted, but when I get going—"

She interrupted. "Please, Spencer? I'm trying to get comfortable with the idea of this, but you're not making it easy."

"It'd be plenty easy," he groused, "if you'd swing with it a little. This doesn't have to be all work, y'know."

"But it does. The only reason we're doing it is so I can have a baby. It's not like we *feel* anything for each other."

"We don't have to *feel* anything to be able to enjoy each other's bodies. I liked touching your breast. I might just like touching the rest of you, and the feeling may be mutual. I'm told I'm a decent lover."

"I'm sure you're a wonderful lover, but I can't play games." Feeling vulnerable, she whispered, "Please, Spencer? I've agreed to do things your way because I want this baby more than anything, but I can't pretend this is something it's not. I want everything we do to be honest. Please?"

Spencer stared at her for a long time. Finally, looking rebellious but determined, he got to his feet. "I'll be here on the sixth. If there's any change in the plan, you know how to reach me." Without another word, he left.

5

THE SIXTH OF JULY fell on a Saturday. Given a choice, Jenna would have had it fall on a weekday, when she could busy herself at McCue's from morning to night and thereby keep her nervousness about being with Spencer in check. But her ovaries knew nothing about apprehension. They operated the same as always. Her temperature followed its established pattern, staying well below normal in prelude to a dip on the eighth.

Spencer called on Friday morning before she left for work. "Just wanted to confirm our date," he said.

"It's not a date," Jenna chided. "It's an appointment." She was determined to keep things on the up-and-up regarding the exact nature of their liaison. Spencer hadn't chosen her as a lover. She couldn't pretend that he had—and she couldn't let *him* think she was pretending it. That would be humiliating. Things were awkward enough without it.

"Appointment, then," he conceded in a deep but agreeable voice. "Are we on?"

"Yes."

"Good." Nonchalantly, he said, "I made an appointment to have some work done on the plane. The best mechanic around is at Norwood Airport, which is about an hour's drive from your place. Feel like taking a ride and picking me up there tomorrow afternoon?"

"Uh, sure."

"That way we can talk a little before we—well, we can talk."

For a split second Jenna imagined that he was feeling awkward himself. Then she ruled out the possibility. Spencer wouldn't feel awkward about sex. He was too experienced for that.

"Sounds fine," she said, managing to sound fully composed. "What time should I be there?"

"I won't be able to leave here until afternoon. Allowing for air traffic, then time to make sure my guy knows what I want done—is six-thirty too late?"

She felt instant relief. "Six-thirty's fine." That meant she *could* keep herself busy all day, and it meant that she'd only have to worry about entertaining Spencer on Sunday. On Monday morning, she'd be back at work.

"Drive right around to Hangar C," he instructed, "and give a honk to let me know you're there. See you then."

"Okay. 'Bye."

HE LOOKED UNFAIRLY dashing. He was wearing a navy shirt with the cuffs rolled and the tails out, and khaki shorts that left his long legs bare to his deck shoes. He had a worn-looking duffel thrown over his shoulder and a bulging briefcase under his arm, and might have been mistaken for a weekending yuppie if it hadn't been for the carved lines of his face. They were bold and lent him an untamed look, upheld by his scar, his dark tan and his even darker, windblown hair. And then there were his eyes, always his eyes.

With a helpless sigh and more than a flutter inside, Jenna waved and waited while he crossed the tarmac to where the Jaguar was parked. She half expected him to come to the driver's side and shoo her over. Instead he opened the passenger door, tossed his gear into the back and slid in.

"Sorry," he muttered, and stared out the front. "The goddamn mechanic forgot I'd called, and he took off for the weekend. His partner was there, but he doesn't know his ass from his elbow. He's not touching *my* plane."

"So what will you do?"

"Mac'll be back on Monday. He'll have to do the work then." He looked at her. "Have you been waiting long?"

"Five minutes. It was nothing." She couldn't take her eyes from his. They were as intense as ever, yet distracted. "You look tired. Was it a difficult flight?"

"The flight was okay. It was everything I had to do beforehand. My editor doesn't like my latest manuscript and wants major revisions. That news came in the mail yesterday—the bastard couldn't tell me in person. I spent most of the afternoon on the phone with him. We were able to compromise on some of the stuff, but there's still a hell of a lot to be done. I'll have to work on it here."

Jenna couldn't believe her luck. She'd been granted a reprieve in the entertainment department. "That's fine. You can work in my office at home. There's a huge desk and good light." She would bend over backward to be accommodating. "Do you need a computer?"

He made a disparaging sound. "I can barely type, let alone use a computer."

She was amazed. Spencer always had such a capable air about him that she had assumed he was proficient in just about everything.

"Don't look at me that way," he told her. "I've been on the go since I was twenty-two, and computers only came in big after that. When would I have the time to learn to use one? I've always done just fine paying a typist." He scowled. "But let me tell you, revisions are a pain in the butt."

"When do they have to be done?"

"Last week."

"Oops."

His scowl faded. "Yeah. Oops." His mouth curved into a lopsided smile, and his eyes did focus on her then. They seemed suddenly warmer, then warmer still and filled with sexual innuendo.

Jenna tore her gaze away, only to have it land on his legs, which were nearly as compelling.

"Problem with the shorts?" he asked. "I'll have you know that in the middle of all that garbage with my editor, I kept thinking about what to wear today. Totally aside from the fact that it's summer and the plane can get warm, I thought it'd be good for you to see my legs so they won't be such a shock later on."

She forced herself to look more casually at the appendages in question. They were well formed, firm and long, as tanned as his face but hairy. "I've seen men's legs before. In fact, I've seen yours before."

He frowned. "When?"

"The summer between college and business school. Don't you remember? Caroline and I were traveling through the Greek islands. You met us on Crete."

"Oh, yeah," he said with a smile that spread over his face as memory returned. "I made you call home first thing, because neither of you had bothered to call the parents and they were frantic—which *I* knew because I'd had the misfortune to call home about something else entirely, and they let *me* have it like I was the one who was lost!"

"We weren't lost. We just couldn't get to a phone."

He snickered. "I've used that excuse too many times myself to buy it. You didn't *want* to call home. But, hey—" he raised a forgiving hand "—I can understand that. It was the first time you'd been away alone. The freedom you felt was heady."

Jenna smiled at the memory. "It was that." She took a breath. "Anyway, you spent a couple of days with us, mostly at the beach. So I've seen your legs."

"You've seen a lot more if you were at the beach with me."

"You were wearing a bathing suit."

"Not much of one, if I correctly remember those days."

He did. His bathing suit had been small and sleek. Jenna remembered admiring him in it, but that was all she'd done. He was Caroline's elder brother, twenty-eight to her twenty-two, and though they came from similar backgrounds, he lived such a different life from Jenna that she never dreamed there might be any entanglement between them.

There certainly was now, and those long, tanned, hair-spattered legs made her all the more aware of it. She cleared her throat. "Yes. Well." Praying that driving would distract her from his imposing presence, she started the car. "Do you want to go back to the house and drop your things off?"

"I'd rather eat. I'm starved." He was scanning the stores and businesses that lined the road. "There used to be a terrific steak place around here—Terry's, Carrie's—"

"Corey's?"

"That's it. Is it still open?"

"Uh-huh. Want to go?"

"A-S-A-P."

In less than ten minutes, they were at the restaurant, but it was nearly forty minutes before they were seated and another forty minutes before their food arrived. Jenna saw the expectant looks Spencer sent their waitress and waited for him to explode at the delay the way some other men would have. But he didn't. He shifted in his seat and went through two baskets of rolls, but he didn't complain about the wait. Instead, he kept Jenna talking about McCue's, about people they both knew, about Caroline and the kids.

When the food arrived, he ate his own, plus half of what Jenna left on her plate. "I need all the energy I can get," he explained with a mischievous look.

"Spencer," she complained.

"What?"

"That's embarrassing."

"Sorry. I couldn't resist."

Wiping the smugness from his face, he finished eating. Jenna arched a brow when he refused dessert, but they both had coffee, and when the waitress brought the check, she reached for it first.

Spencer's hand flattened hers to the table. With his other hand, he pulled the check free. "I pay."

"That's not right. You're here on my account. I want to pay."

"*I pay*," he repeated in such a firm voice that she backed off. More gently, almost distractedly as he pulled out his charge card, he added, "Besides, I ate twice as much as you."

Not wanting to risk another reference to why that was so, Jenna sat silently while he settled the bill. It was dark outside by the time they returned to the car.

The darkness did nothing to ease her nerves. Spencer had said they would do it at night, and it was night. Jenna couldn't forget that for a minute during the drive to Little Compton. Hands tight at ten and two on the wheel, she kept picturing her house, picturing the bed she had freshened up for Spencer, then picturing her own bed and wondering which one they would use.

Spencer seemed deep in thought, as well. Once, passing beneath a streetlight, she saw that he had his elbow braced on the door and his forehead braced on his fingertips, and for an instant, she worried that he was changing his mind.

"Everything okay?" she asked.

"Yeah."

She hesitated, then said, "You sound angry."

"Not angry." He was silent for a minute. Then he sighed, dropped his hand to his thigh and looked out the windshield. "Unsure."

Her heart beat harder against her ribs. "Unsure about whether you want to go ahead with it?"

"Unsure about *how* to go ahead with it. I've seduced women plenty of times, but you don't want to be seduced. You want this to be businesslike. I've never done it that way."

On a ray of hope, she said, "Y'know, we could still do it my way. I'm sure my doctor would be willing to meet us in his office tomorrow—"

"Forget it," Spencer stated. He didn't have to elaborate. The finality of his tone said it all.

Jenna knew better than to ignore the message. Yes, she wished they were doing it her way, but still, Spencer was doing her a huge favor. He was helping her make a baby. A baby. She couldn't forget that.

"It shouldn't be difficult," she said in a deferential tone. If he didn't know what to do, it was really the blind leading the blind. "We both know the mechanics. Isn't that enough?"

He didn't answer. In fact, he didn't say anything for the rest of the drive, which saddened Jenna. Always in the past when she'd been with him, talk had been easy. She loved hearing about his travels, his adventures, his books, and as though sensing her interest, he relaxed in the telling. But the air between them was tense now. She had the awful thought that their relationship might be permanently changed, and prayed that wouldn't be so.

When she pulled up at the house, he grabbed his gear from the back seat and followed her in. She wavered for an instant in the hall before saying, "I'll, uh, show you to your room. You may want to unpack." She led him up the stairs and down the hall. The room she had chosen for him was nearly as large as her own, though at the opposite end of the house. At the door, she moved aside to let him pass.

He went in, dropped his things on the bed and stood with his hands on his hips and his back to her. His spine was straight, his displeasure evident.

"If you don't like this room . . ." she began, only to stop when he turned quickly. His face was dark, his eyes iridescent as they held her in their thrall.

"I think we should do it now, since neither of us will relax till it's done. I need a shower. I'll meet you in your room in ten minutes, okay?"

Jenna knew he was right. The longer they put it off, the more nervous she would be, and she was plenty nervous already. At his words, she had started to shake. It was all she could do not to let it show.

"Fifteen minutes," she bargained, then swallowed and explained, "It takes me longer. In the shower."

"Fifteen minutes," he agreed. His eyes held hers for a heart-stopping moment more before letting her go.

SPENCER TOOK HIS TIME in the shower. Long after he had soaped himself from head to toe, he stood with the hot spray concentrated on the tight muscles at the back of his neck. True, the mess with the manuscript had gotten him down, but he suspected that he might have handled it better if Jenna hadn't been weighing heavy on his mind.

No artificial insemination, he had told her with such smugness. *It's the real thing or nothing.* Such arrogance. *Sexual intercourse, between you and me.* Such cocksureness, and why the hell not? He was a handsome guy. He was a super lover. He would show little Jenna McCue the time of her life, and she'd get the baby she wanted, to boot.

He had believed all that up until several days earlier, when the reality of what he had arranged had hit him— and it wasn't the baby part that bothered him, as much as the Jenna part. She was Caroline's best friend, and he had always liked her. She was gentle and understanding. She accepted his way of life. She was also vulnerable where men were concerned, something he hadn't realized until she had put her proposal to him at his parents' anniversary party.

He wasn't used to vulnerable women, any more than he was used to petite women. He was used to women who were tall and shapely, who reveled in their sexuality, who came to him with confidence and hunger, and demanded as much as they gave.

Jenna wasn't like those women at all, but now he felt a responsibility for her. He wanted to please her, but he wasn't sure how best to do it. She wanted their coming together to be a simple, straightforward coupling for the sole purpose of producing a child. His body wanted more.

He shifted to put the force of the spray on the small of his back, then raised first one arm, then the other to stretch his muscles. He supposed he could find a compromise. He could be gentle, without dwelling on preliminaries. He could make her feel good if she let him. The question was whether she would.

Turning the water off, he reached for the towel and dried himself. He looked at his foggy reflection in the mirror, pushed his hair around a little, took a toothbrush from his grooming kit and set about brushing his teeth, and all the while he pictured Jenna in her own bathroom getting ready for him. By the time he'd rinsed his mouth, a slow heat was gathering between his legs.

No, getting it up wouldn't be a problem. Preparing Jenna to take it in might be.

He glanced at his watch. It was time. Knotting a dry towel around his waist, he left the bathroom and headed down the hall. Jenna's was the only other room lit. He assumed it had once been her parents' room, but he wasn't thinking about her parents when he came to stand at the door. A single low light glowed by the turned-down bed. She was beside it, with her back to him. She was wearing a robe that was long and white, and her head was bowed. Only when he came closer did he see that she was studying something in her hand.

"Whatcha got?" he asked softly.

She held up a tiny bracelet made of glass beads interspersed with ones of ivory that spelled out her name.

"My parents had this made when I was a baby. I always loved it. If I have a little girl, I want to give her one with her name on it, too."

Spencer looked at the bracelet for a minute, before his gaze was drawn up to Jenna. Her hair was dark as the night, spilling softly around her face and onto her shoulders. Her skin was moist, her cheeks a pale pink. She smelled of spring flowers and looked incredibly young.

He touched her hair. "I think that sounds like a nice idea." He ran his fingers through the loose waves.

She tucked her chin lower. The gesture made him feel that much larger beside her and more protective. Gently he took the bracelet from her hand and set it on the table by the bed. While he was there, he switched off the light. "If it were up to me," he said, straightening close by her side, "I'd leave it on. But I think you'll be more comfortable this way."

"Yes," she whispered. "Thank you."

He touched her sleeve. "Is there a nightgown under this?"

She nodded.

He kept his voice low and gentle. "Want to take the robe off?"

Head still bent, she slipped the silky fabric from her shoulders. In a strained voice that sounded as if she were trying for humor but missed, she said, "Right about now, the nurse would be handing me a paper sheet, telling me to take everything off from the waist down and climb on the table."

"No table here. No paper sheet." Spencer paused. In an even lower voice, he said, "Is there anything you need to take off from the waist down?"

She shook her head.

That bit of information sent a spark from his brain to his groin. Needing to touch her, he curved a hand around her neck. At the same time, he lowered his head to her hair to breathe in the sweet scent of roses.

She slipped away from him. Climbing into bed, she moved to the far side and slid down against the pillow.

The room was dark, but Spencer's eyes had adjusted enough to see the tension in her body as she lay waiting for him. His first impulse was to stand there debating what to do next, but if he hesitated for long, she would remind him that they could go to the doctor's office in the morning, and he wouldn't, couldn't do that. It went against his grain. And his groin. He was already aroused.

Coming down on a knee, he crawled across the queen-size bed until his thigh met Jenna's hip. He touched her face and whispered, "There's nothing to be afraid of."

"I'm not afraid," she whispered back.

He traced her jaw. "Then tense."

"I just want this to work so badly."

"It will if you relax. I can help you do that." He slipped his hand to her neck, then her throat.

Her eyes were wide in the dark. "You don't have to, Spence. Really. I'm okay. I'm really fine."

"Well, I'm not," he said, taking a different tactic. Climbing under the bedcovers, he stretched out on his side, facing her. "I want you now, want you badly—"

"You don't have to say that."

"It's the truth." Needing to show her, he rolled on top of her and let her feel the full weight of his lower body. He knew he'd made his point when she took in a quick breath. "Believe me?"

"I believe you."

"Then relax your legs a little so I can feel you where I'm supposed to."

"This is so embarrassing, Spencer," she murmured, but she did as he asked. She caught in another breath when he settled more snugly against her.

"Feel okay?" he asked.

"Feels okay," she answered.

"I'm supposed to be on top, aren't I?"

"Yes. I'll lose . . . less. This is *so* embarrassing."

"No, it isn't. It's nice." He moved gently against her. "I don't know why I didn't think of it sooner."

Her voice was more breathy. "You didn't think of it because I'm not your type."

"If you're not my type, why am I so hard? And besides, how would you know what my type is?"

"Caroline tells me."

"Caroline knows diddly-squat." He was wondering if he knew much more, since he had known Jenna all these years without seeing the possibilities, but that was water over the dam. Carefully holding his upper body weight from her, he said, "I'm afraid I'll hurt you if you're not ready, so I'm going to touch you now, Jenna. Just a little. I know you don't want to get into things this way, but if I hurt you, I won't be able to go on. I want you to feel good, too."

"I don't need that."

"But I do." He lowered his head to her neck and kissed the warm skin there, kissed it lightly, then, without planning to, more deeply, because her scent did something to him. That something was strong enough to startle him. His muscles were trembling faintly when he raised his head. "Jeez."

She was instantly alarmed. "What's wrong?"

He laughed, then growled. "Nothing." He buried his face against her neck and undulated helplessly against her. He couldn't believe how aroused he was. He supposed it could be because he hadn't had a woman in a while, but he'd had dry stretches before without this sudden, dire wanting. Against her neck, he warned, "I don't know how long I can hold off, Jenna."

Her arms, which had been lying still until then, crept around his back. Her fingers dug into his muscles. "Don't wait. Don't wait. Do it now."

But he had to know if she was ready. So he ran a hand down her side and came up under her nightgown. The feel of her smooth, bare thigh against his palm was like fire, but no more so than the unevenness of her breathing. That, too, had crept up on him. It was the most welcome sound in the world just then.

"Are you okay?" he whispered hoarsely.

Breathlessly, she whispered back, "I'm okay."

He touched her between her legs, and a tiny sound came from the back of her throat. "You're sweet," he murmured. "So sweet." He stroked her, gently finding his way deeper. Well after he had the answer he sought, he continued to rub her. "I want to kiss you, Jenna."

"No!"

"Your mouth." He lowered his head to hers, but her high-pitched plea stopped him short.

"Don't, Spencer, please don't. Kissing makes it something it's not." She paused and let out an involuntary kind of hum. At the same time, albeit in a motion so subtle as to missed by a lesser lover, she moved her hips against his hand.

Spencer wanted to argue, but she was ready for him, and, Lord knew, he was ready for her. Taking his hands from her only long enough to drag the towel from his

hips, he tangled his legs with hers, spreading them farther apart, and positioned himself at their notch. He
reached for her hands and held them on either side of
her head. Then he watched her closely while he pushed
forward into her warmth.

She was tight. Wonderfully tight. He let out a sigh
and grinned down at her. "How does it feel?"

"Full."

"It is that." His grin persisted. It stretched wider in
an agony of pleasure when he withdrew and thrust forward again. He moaned this time and with a steady
downward pressure deepened his penetration. "Jenna,
oh, Lord, Jenna," he whispered. He wanted to laugh,
or hug her, or yank up her nightgown and put his hands
all over her. Instead, with another moan, he said, "This
feels so good."

"I'm not too short?"

He did give a laugh then, a low, throaty sound. "Hell,
no. We fit—" he took a shaky breath "—very well." As
though to prove it, he slid against her inside and out.

She let out a tiny gasp. "I'm glad." Her hands came
around to his front, palms grazing his nipples, then returning there when he sucked in a great gulp of air. "I
want a baby, Spencer," she cried. "Give me one, please,
give me one?"

The reminder of her purpose should have doused at
least some of Spencer's flame, but it didn't. Quite the
opposite happened. He felt a heat so sudden and intense that he nearly came apart. Yielding to the demand of his body, he moved against Jenna with a hard,
driving rhythm that gained in speed and depth until,
with a last, forceful thrust and a near-savage cry, he
erupted inside her.

His orgasm went on and on. He was panting and damp with sweat when he finally collapsed on top of her, and even then, he kept his buttocks locked so that he could stay deep inside her until the last bit of pulsing pleasure was done. Finally, after several long, air-thirsty breaths, he rolled to the side.

Jenna was on her back, her head turned to look at him. Even in the dark, he could see the expectancy on her face. He knew she was thinking of the baby, and felt a glimmer of disappointment. His ego had wanted her to be bowled over by his lovemaking, so much so that she forgot the reason behind it. But, then, she had worked hard to keep that reason in her mind. Perhaps it was for the best.

With a gentle hand, he unbunched the nightgown from her waist and lowered it to her thighs. When that was done, he put his fingertips to her lips. Then he cleared his throat. "So. Did we do it? Did you feel that little spark when egg met sperm?"

She was lying so quietly and was so long in answering that he wondered if something was wrong. He was about to ask when, in a small voice, she said, "There isn't any little spark, at least not one I'd be able to feel."

"Do you feel any different?"

"I don't know."

"What does that mean?"

Lying very still, she said, "It means that I feel different, but I don't know whether it has to do with the baby or not."

"If not, what would it be from?"

It was a while before she said, in an even smaller voice, "What we just did."

Spencer felt a light jab inside. Rolling to his stomach, he propped himself on his elbows with his head inches from hers. "Was it any good, Jenna?"

"It was great," she said with a burst of enthusiasm. "You were incredible. I mean, if any man can make me pregnant—"

"For you," he interrupted, and put a hand on her stomach. "Was it good for you? Did you feel good down here?" He started to move his hand lower, but she grabbed it and held it still.

"It felt nice." She paused, then admitted, "Better than I thought it would."

"Why did you think it wouldn't?" he asked. He'd been wondering about that a lot, wondering why someone like Jenna hadn't had terrific experiences with men. "I told you once that it had to be the guys, and I believe that now more than ever, since I sure as hell can't find a thing wrong with *you*. But why were you expecting the worst with me?"

"I wasn't expecting the worst. It's just that I wasn't doing it for the pleasure of it."

"But there was some?"

"Yes," she said softly.

He was relieved to hear that. His own pleasure had been so intense that he was feeling very selfish. "I wish there had been more. Can I do it for you now?" He tried to move his hand lower, but she tightened her hold on it.

"No. I'm fine. Really, Spencer."

"I'd like to."

She gave a short shake of her head.

"Then let me hold you, at least," he said, and was reaching to pull her into his arms, when she gave a small cry and put a protesting hand on his chest.

"I'm supposed to lie flat for a few minutes. The less I move, the greater the chance of something getting where it's supposed to be."

Spencer could understand that argument, but he was feeling a need that wasn't to be denied. "Okay," he said agreeably, and hoisted himself up. He punched and pushed at the pillows until they were arranged to his satisfaction. Then he arranged himself in such a way that he could slip an arm under Jenna and bring her against him without moving her lower body an inch. "If the mountain won't come to Muhammad," he said with a sigh.

"You don't have to do this, Spencer. It's not part of the deal. You have work to do. Don't feel that you have to lie here—"

He covered her mouth with a hand. "If I wanted to work, I'd work. If I wanted to get up, I'd get up. Trust me, Jenna." He removed his hand.

"But—"

He put his hand right back. "Good Lord, you're like a broken record! Yes, I know that I'm only here to help you make a baby and that anything else is unnecessary, but I want to hold you—I just want to hold you. Unless you really don't want to be held. In which case I'll crawl off to the corner and lie there in a pathetic heap until I recover enough of my strength to crawl back down the hall. In case you've forgotten, I've just given you every bit of the life in me!"

Jenna relaxed against him. "Not every bit," she scolded, but with good humor. "You've got enough left to argue."

"Barely."

She made a sound against his chest. He felt her breath stir the hair there, and was stunned when the stirring echoed deep inside him.

"Jenna?"

"Yes?"

"Are you feeling less embarrassed now?"

"A little."

"There was really nothing to be embarrassed about."

"There was. You're you."

"And you're you, but I'm not embarrassed."

"Men are more cavalier about things like this."

"Like having a baby? Are you kidding?"

"I was talking about having sex. You'll be able to go downstairs for breakfast tomorrow morning like nothing at all happened. It may be harder for me."

"And so it should. Something did happen. But that doesn't mean seeing each other has to be hard."

She drew in a deep, faintly shaky breath. When it left her, it stirred him again. "When you do that," he said in a low voice that held equal parts humor and warning, "I start thinking about all those things under your nightgown that I want to feel clearly but can't." He turned himself so that she could clearly feel what that thinking was doing to him. With his mouth by her ear, he said, "How long do you have to lie here?"

"A little longer."

"Can we do it again then?"

"No. We have to wait until Monday."

"But I want you again now."

"Spencer."

"I do. Can't you feel it?" he asked, knowing that she had to, since his arousal was heavy against her groin.

"We have to wait until Monday, Spencer. That way we'll be optimizing the chances of conception."

She was missing the point. She was deliberately turning a deaf ear to the fact that he found her attractive, and one part of Spencer wanted to shake her hard. The other part just wanted to make love to her again, to feel that intense pleasure again, to give her a taste of it this time.

Since neither part was going to win out—and since he did understand the importance of her lying still—he let it go. He could live until Monday, he supposed. He guessed he'd have to.

6

JENNA AWOKE on Sunday morning to the lingering scent of Spencer in her bed. Burying her face in the pillow, she breathed it in. She rolled over, taking the pillow with her, and, eyes still closed, held it close as she remembered the events of the previous night.

Her insides tingled. She put her hand to her stomach and wondered whether, indeed, there was the beginnings of a baby inside. The thought brought her down to earth with a reminder of what she was supposed to be doing. Taking the thermometer from the night stand, she put it under her tongue. Five minutes later, satisfied, she returned it to its case.

The timing was right. Her ovaries were about to release an egg, and an army of sperm was waiting right there to fertilize it. The conditions were optimal. Her doctor would be pleased.

Smiling softly, she lay back, and in that instant, felt more peaceful than ever before. In the next moment, she felt a burst of energy. Pushing the sheets aside, she climbed out of bed and headed for the bathroom.

By the time she emerged, she had showered, knotted her hair back and made up her face—none of which she would normally have done on a lazy Sunday at home. But there was nothing normal about this Sunday. She had a house guest, one whom she wanted to impress with her poise, her maturity and her competence. To that end, she bypassed her usual shorts and T-shirt in favor of a more sophisticated pair of narrow white pants, a long navy blouse that she belted at the hip and navy flats.

She listened at the door for sounds of Spencer but heard nothing. He had been up late the night before—she had heard him moving around the house—and was still sleeping, she assumed. Grateful for that, she tiptoed down the stairs and into the kitchen, where, as quietly as possible, she put coffee on to brew. She had just closed the lid and was turning around, when the sudden sight of his large figure made her jump.

Gasping, she pressed a hand to her heart. "I didn't hear you."

He was standing barefooted in the doorway, wearing an old sweatshirt and sweatpants. A dark stubble covered his jaw, lessening the effect of his scar. He looked sleepy and mussed and thoroughly endearing. He also looked unabashedly masculine—so that even if she hadn't smelled him on her sheets, even if she hadn't thought of him during her shower, even if she *hadn't* been thoroughly intimate with him the night before, she would have felt his pull. It helped some that his eyes were half-lidded; if those electric blues had been open wide, she might have melted on the spot. Her cheeks were heated enough as it was.

In an attempt to buy time to calm down, she tugged open the refrigerator and peered inside. She had gone to the market on Saturday and was well stocked. "Would you like an omelet? I have some terrific Vermont cheddar to put in it. Or ham. Or onions. Or all of the above." She straightened, took a half step back and bumped into him. Her head shot around, eyes up to his. "Sorry. I didn't hear you come over." She ducked into the refrigerator. "If you'd rather have bagels and cream cheese, I have those, or you can have an omelet *and* a bagel—"

"Jenna."

She set a carton of orange juice on the counter. "Hmm?"

"Look at me, Jenna."

She darted him another quick glance before going back for the butter. "Pancakes, maybe?"

He put his hands on her shoulders and physically turned her. "Jenna, *look* at me."

That was the last thing she wanted to do. Looking at him would bring back the image of what they'd done in bed, and that image made her squirm. But she wasn't a coward. Mustering the composure that stood her well as president and chairman of the board of McCue's, she tipped up her chin and met his gaze.

"You're still embarrassed," he accused.

"A little."

"But why?"

She knew he was mystified. What was a little sex to him? He had made love to more women in his day than she had *dated* men. He was freer with his body, and more confident in it than she would ever be in hers. He wouldn't understand the discomfort she felt knowing he was Caroline's big brother, the awe she felt knowing he was a world-renowned adventurer and author. He was larger than life, and though she was successful and sophisticated within her own sphere, that sphere was narrow. His was not.

But she didn't want to go into all that. So she said, "The husband of one of my good friends is a gynecologist. Sharon can't understand why I don't use him, but there's no way I could. Some things demand detachment. If Don were my doctor, each and every time I saw

him, whether it was at a cookout here, at a party
somewhere else, at the movies, the post office or the
supermarket, I'd know—we'd *both* know—what he'd
seen and touched. I'd be mortified." She paused, then
added, "Having sex with you is a little like that. You're
not my lover. You're my...my...I don't know *what* to
call you."

Spencer scowled. "I didn't see a hell of a lot. It was
dark."

"You touched."

"And enjoyed." He gave her small shake. "So there's
no cause for mortification. You should be proud, Jenna.
What we did last night felt really good!"

She wanted to believe him. She wanted to believe that
he wasn't just saying that to keep her spirits up. He was
capable of it, she knew. She had seen the way he had
buoyed Caroline when, soon after her wedding, she
was convinced that her marriage was on the rocks.
Ironic, given that he was against marriage for himself,
but he had argued a wonderful case for patience, understanding and compromise. Caroline had listened
and stuck with it. Her marriage had survived that rocky
start and grown strong.

Oh, yes, Spencer could be convincing. Jenna wanted
to believe every last word he said. Somehow, though,
she didn't think it would be wise. A woman could become addicted to praise like that, and Spencer would
soon be gone.

With that in mind, she said, "I'm really grateful for
all you're doing, Spencer. I hope you know how much.
My baby is going to be so wonderful, and I have you to
thank."

His blue eyes scolded her for trying to change the
subject. "You can thank me by relaxing when I'm

around. You can also thank me by looking a little messy once in a while. You didn't have to get all spiffed up."

"I'm not all spiffed up."

He looked her over. "Silk blouse? Hair in a twist? Makeup?" He challenged her with an arched brow. "On a Sunday morning?"

She was silent in her guilt.

"I know what you're doing, Jenna. You're trying to keep this thing businesslike, but some things don't have anything to do with business, and this is one. Sure, what we're doing is unconventional. It's an arrangement, something we agreed to for a specific purpose, but that doesn't mean it has to be cold or matter-of-fact. You can't be detached when it comes to something like this. There are feelings and emotions involved." He gave her another gentle shake. "I won't have you stifling them, do you hear?"

"I can't help but hear," she said softly.

"But will you *listen*?"

"I'll try."

He stared at her for another minute before raising his hands in concession. "Okay. That sounds okay."

She hadn't expected him to let her off the hook so easily. The fact that he had, gave her a boost. "So what do you want for breakfast?"

Without a moment's thought, he reeled off, "One omelet loaded, plus a bagel, but no pancakes, and I can help make the omelet. I've been cooking for myself for years."

She wasn't surprised. Spencer was the most independent man she knew. "That may be, but you're in my house, as my guest, doing me a monumental favor. You wouldn't let me pay for dinner last night. The least I can do is to make you breakfast. Besides, if you don't let me do it, you'll never know what kind of a cook I'll be for your child."

She knew she'd made her point when he raised his hands again, this time in surrender. "Make me breakfast. I'll take a shower while you do. As soon as I eat, I have to work."

JENNA WASN'T SURE what she'd expected, but it certainly wasn't the doggedness with which Spencer sat in her office and worked on his book. She had thought he'd take breaks. She had thought he'd keep tabs on what she was doing. She had thought he would pace the floor, brooding over one passage or another. But he sat still, pencil in hand, barely moving from his chair all morning.

At first, she sat on the back patio reading the Sunday paper, expecting him to join her at any minute. She made sure that her blouse didn't bunch at the waist, that she wasn't caught reading the funnies, that her legs were gracefully arranged. When minutes became hours and she realized her efforts were wasted, she began doing the things she would normally do on a Sunday. She changed the sheets and put the old ones in the wash. She went through her closet for clothes to be dropped off at the dry cleaner the next day. She caught up on personal correspondence. She called her marketing director to discuss an upcoming advertising program.

She waited for Spencer to emerge at lunchtime. When he didn't, she brought him a large turkey sandwich and a soda. He finished both in record time, refused seconds, and left the office only long enough to use the bathroom before going back to work.

He did take time off for dinner, but not until eight o'clock that night and then only for pizza in the kitchen.

Jenna was oddly disappointed. She had wanted to cook, but he argued that he was too preoccupied to appreciate the effort and that pizza would do just fine. So she called in an order and brought it home, then, while he ate, asked questions about his book. It was about a trek he had made through the rain forests of the Amazon in search of a tribe of Indians that was reportedly using medicinal plants to cure certain cancers. While the efficacy of those plants had yet to be proven, the core of Spencer's story consisted of the Indians' way of life.

"When can I read it?" Jenna asked. His enthusiasm, so rich in his tone and expression, was contagious.

"When it's published next spring."

"Not before?"

He shook his head. "No one reads it before, except my editor." He made a face. "Not that he's ever gonna like this one." He carried his plate to the sink. "I have a feeling he'll fight me all the way. He was looking for a treasure hunt. I gave him an anthropological study. He can say he doesn't like the way the story's organized, but that's just an excuse."

"What does he have against an anthropological study?"

"It's not a treasure hunt."

"But it could be fascinating."

"It *is* fascinating—" Spencer snorted "—but to convince him of that is something else." He added her plate to the dishwasher and closed the door. "Okay, I'm back to work."

"You've never done an anthropological study before," Jenna said, turning to let her voice follow him as he left the room.

"Yeah, well, it's time," he called back before he disappeared from sight.

She wanted to ask him more, but the office swallowed him up. So she brought him coffee and kept his cup refilled, then baked brownies and offered him those. By eleven, realizing that there wasn't much more she could do for him, she decided to go to bed. Going to the office door, she waited until he reached a break point and looked up. "I think I'll turn in. Should I put on a fresh pot of coffee?"

He sat back in his chair and regarded her with tired eyes. "Nah. I've had enough to keep me up for a while. What time do you leave tomorrow?"

"Seven-fifteen. I have an appointment at eight. Will you be working here all day?"

With a despairing glance at the papers that covered the desk in clumps, he nodded. "When will you be back?"

A buzzing started in the pit of her stomach. Tomorrow night was the night. Again. "Five-thirty. Would you like to eat in or out?"

"Out. I'll be stir-crazy by then. But I don't want to bump into my parents or Caroline—" He interrupted himself to ask, "Does Caroline know I'm here?"

"I didn't tell her. I thought you would if you wanted to."

"That would have made you more uncomfortable. Has she asked you what I decided to do?"

"Yes, but I told her we were still discussing it."

"Once you're pregnant, will you tell her the truth?"

"I'm not sure," Jenna said, then added softly, "probably not. That might be easier all the way around." She went on before he could comment. "So where would you like to go to dinner?"

"Someplace where we won't bump into anyone who will want to talk for three hours. And I don't want to dress up. Any suggestions?"

"I'll think of a place," she promised, and raised a casual hand. "'Night." She slipped away from the door.

"Jenna?" She leaned back in to find his eyes suddenly less tired-looking than they had been moments earlier. They were warmer, more direct and penetrating. They sent an unmistakable message, which he followed up with "I'll look forward to it."

Keeping her poise, she simply nodded and left, but she thought about his words all the way back to her room. She thought of them later, when she lay in bed ignoring the book on her lap. They were the last things she thought about before she fell asleep and the first things she thought about when she woke up in the morning. When her thermometer told her that she was ovulating, the words took on a more practical meaning. Even that, though, she pushed from her mind when she set off for work.

She was busy all morning, going from one meeting to the next. When she had a break at noontime, she found herself wondering how Spencer was doing. The telephone beckoned, but she resisted. Theirs was a business relationship, she reminded herself, and she didn't call business associates to see if they'd eaten lunch.

So she didn't call Spencer, but went back to work, and for a while, she successfully immersed herself in studying the company's latest spreadsheets. As the afternoon wore on, however, her mind began to wander, and always in the same direction. She thought of Spencer coming to her again, of his touching her, of the heat of his skin and the heaviness of his sex. She grew warm inside, then trembly. She actually left the office early and drove around for an hour to relax before going home.

Spencer was sound asleep when she arrived. After searching the house for him, she found him on the patio, sprawled facedown on the chaise longue. His bare feet hung over the end. One arm was tucked under him, the other bent to the flagstone, long fingers loosely splayed. She debated waking him, but didn't have the heart. So she called the restaurant—a dark, quiet place in Providence where neither of them would have been recognized—and canceled their reservations. Then she changed into a casual sun dress and, leaving a note on the counter lest he wake up while she was gone, went to the local market for a pound of fresh shrimp.

Spencer was still sleeping when she returned, which pleased her tremendously. She liked the idea that he was getting the rest that he needed. She also liked the idea of making dinner, which was amusing in that she was a businesswoman, not a cook—but understandable given the maternal instincts that had taken her over in recent days. Granted, Spencer wasn't a child, but the urge to nurture was there. She looked on what she was doing as practice.

With three separate cookbooks open on the counter, she made shrimp curry, saffron rice and a cucumber salad. When Spencer slept on, she took out a fourth cookbook and whipped up a cold strawberry soup, and when she still had time to spare, she made an apple crunch for dessert. By then the sun had set, and she was wondering whether he was all right. So she went out to the darkened patio and knelt beside him. Only one eye was in sight, and it was closed. The scar running along his jaw was masked by the night and less threatening than usual. In fact, the whole of him looked less threatening than usual. He actually looked vulnerable.

Not sure whether she liked the vulnerable Spencer over the one who was in full command, she finger-combed the hair from his brow and rested a hand on his back. His skin was warm through his T-shirt, his muscles firm to the touch. "Spencer?" she called softly. "Spencer?"

He took a deep breath, then seemed to settle into sleep again.

She gave him a tiny shake. "Spencer?"

"Mmm."

She waited to see if he would rouse. Since he clearly wasn't unconscious, if he wanted to sleep longer, she couldn't deny him. Dinner would wait.

She was about to stand, when he took another deep breath, squeezed his eye shut, then opened it a crack. His gaze hit her shoulder and stayed there for as long as it took him to realize what he was looking at. Then it lifted slowly to her face.

He looked dazed. She couldn't help but smile. "I was beginning to think you'd contracted sleeping sickness in the jungle."

"Um-hum," he said, without moving his mouth.

"Were you working all day?"

"Umm."

"And last night?"

"Umm."

"Did you finish the revisions?"

"Almost." He yawned and shifted his head so that he could see her with both eyes. Pulling his free hand from the flagstone, he tucked it under his body. "What time is it?"

"Nearly nine."

He grunted. "You should have woken me sooner."

"You were tired."

"We were supposed to go to dinner."

"That's okay. We can eat here. I've been cooking—"

"After working all day?"

"I'm practicing. I'll have to cook for a baby whether I'm tired or not. Besides, I don't mind cooking. It's a change from my work. Of course, I can't guarantee the results."

"That omelet was great. You're a terrific cook."

"I'm still a novice. I haven't had much practice."

"You didn't do it when you were growing up?"

"We always had a cook."

"Why don't you now?"

"Because it'd be pretentious. And a waste of money. And unnecessary. I don't eat a whole lot."

"Clearly," he murmured. In the dark, his gaze dropped to her shoulders, then her breasts.

"I'm not too thin," she said in self-defense. "If I didn't watch what I eat, I'd get fat."

He frowned. "When you were younger, weren't you a little ..."

"Fat?"

"Not fat."

"Chubby," she put in.

"Not chubby. Solid."

"That's, uh, one way to put it. Our cook was *too* good."

"Made brownies all the time, eh?" he asked.

She remembered the plate she'd brought to him the night before. When she'd left for work, there had been a few brownies left, but they were gone when she returned. Not that Spencer had to worry about his weight. He was lean but solid, which, on a man, was a wonderful thing.

"Yes, she made brownies," Jenna admitted with a sigh, "and lots of other incredibly fattening things. It wasn't until I got into college that I lost weight. By the time I got to graduate school, I was into healthy eating. I had my own apartment then, so it was easy. My tastes were simple. What cooking I did was elementary. It's not much fun cooking for one." Thinking about the pleasure she'd had earlier that night in the kitchen, she said, "It's more fun cooking for two." Then she realized that what she'd said could be taken the wrong way, so she added, "God help this baby if it doesn't like haute cuisine."

Spencer continued to lie quietly, looking at her. With the night muting the electric charge of his eyes, she felt surprisingly comfortable.

"The baby will like anything you make," he said.

"I hope so."

"You'll be a good mother."

She smiled. "I hope so."

The smile was still on her face when his hand came from under him and went to the back of her head. It faded when he tugged out a hairpin. "I like your hair down," he said in a deep voice as he pulled out a second pin.

Her pulse picked up. She wanted to tell him to stop, but the words wouldn't come. She wanted to get up and go back to the kitchen, but her legs wouldn't work. One by one, he discarded hairpins until her hair spilled onto her shoulders. He sifted through the waves, working out small tangles, massaging the place on her scalp where the pins had dug in.

Jenna felt suddenly warmer. "Maybe I should, uh, check on the shrimp."

"Don't. I want you, not the shrimp."

"Me?" Her heart beat more loudly. "Now?"

He curved a hand around her neck. "Come here." A slight pressure knocked her off balance. Taking immediate advantage of that, he pulled her forward, and though she put out a hand to steady herself, before she could do more, she was half under him on the cushion.

"Spencer..."

He touched her lips. "Shh." He slid his palm down her throat to the neckline of her dress. "You look sexy."

"I didn't intend that," she said, then sucked in a breath when he cupped her breast. "Spencer—"

"It's okay, honey, it's okay." He kneaded her right through her sun dress in a way that sent hot flashes through her. She made a small sound when he brushed her beaded nipple with a thumb. "That feels good, does it?"

It felt *incredibly* good. "We can't."

"Can't what?"

She struggled to think. He had shifted to her other breast. After delineating its shape, he opened his hand wide and put his little finger and thumb to both nipples at once. She was robbed of all but the smallest fragment of breath and could only manage a faint "Can't do this here."

"Sure, we can. No one'll see. You own everything for acres around."

"But on the patio?" she cried on a pleading note, because his hand was moving down her body now, leaving fire in its wake. "It's not a bed."

He reached under her dress. "I never make love in the same place twice. Didn't I tell you that?"

"No." She nearly choked on a breath when he touched her where she was hot and wet. "Spencer!"

He grinned. All she could see of it was the gleam of his teeth, it was that dark, but she heard it clear as day in his whisper, and she knew its cause. "Oh, yes, you want me."

"I want a baby."

"Right now you want me." His hand left her to deal with his shorts. "The chemistry is right. You can't deny it."

"I didn't plan this."

"Some of the best things are unplanned." Having freed himself, he tugged at her panties. "Lift up."

She lifted. "I'm not comfortable doing this here."

"You will be when you look back on it." He tossed the panties aside and came down between her legs. Slipping his hands under her bottom, he pulled her to him. "When you have your baby, you'll think back to this and laugh."

"I'll think back and blush—Spencer!"

"There we go. Deep inside." He made a guttural sound that was halfway between a grunt and a hum. "Oh, Lord, oh, Lord, does that feel good."

"I don't believe this."

"Wrap your legs around me, honey. There, ohh, there, isn't that better?"

"On the *patio*."

"I'm not sure how slow I can go. Tell me if I hurt you, okay, sweetheart?"

Jenna didn't hear him at first. Her insides were aflame with a most intense pleasure. She held him tightly with her thighs, then with her arms when she felt she'd go up in smoke.

"You with me?" he asked in a thick rumble that was made ragged by the rhythmic movement of his hips.

Her voice was a wisp. "I shouldn't be."

"But you are. Jeez, what was that?"

"What?"

"You did something inside."

She clenched her muscles again. "This?"

He gave a tortured groan and thrust higher, and it was her turn to groan. The feeling inside her was new and intense. No man had ever excited her this way. She could barely think beyond his hardness, heat and size, and the scent she was coming to recognize as his, maybe theirs. Needing more, she strained against him. Her hands moved through the hair on his chest. She clutched his shoulders and began meeting his thrusts.

Burying his mouth against her throat, he bowed his back and quickened his pace. Wanting to feel him deeper, then deeper still, she raised her legs to his waist. Reality was beginning to slip away from her when, with a hoarse cry, Spencer climaxed.

Loving the triumphant sound of his cry and the feel of his pulsing inside her, Jenna held him tightly. Only with the ebbing of his orgasm did she become aware of an inner expectancy unfulfilled. Then, as though he'd read her mind and understood it, she felt his hand slide between their bodies to the place where they were still joined.

She whispered his name in protest.

"You won't lose anything," he whispered back. His finger found what it was seeking and began to pluck that swollen flesh. "I'll stay inside you to stopper things up."

"No," she whispered, but reality started slipping again. She grabbed at his wrist, wanting to pull him away. Instead, the movement of his finger made her weak with wanting, so that she had to hold on tight or fall. The heat grew in her belly and spread through her body like a fog, dimming all thought of protest. Her breasts rose and fell. She arched mindlessly closer to Spencer, oblivious to the soft sounds of need that came from her throat until, with a choked cry, she exploded with a pleasure so total that the world went a brilliant, blinding white.

JENNA HAD NO IDEA how much later it was when Spencer finally lifted off her. She knew it had been a while. Her breathing was even; the dampness on her skin had dried. She wasn't sure whether she had actually dozed or whether she had simply floated in a stupor of satisfaction that was reinforced by the warmth of his body over hers. But she felt a loss the minute he moved.

"Stay put," he whispered, and groped around for her panties. After he had helped her put them on, he fixed his own pants. Then, before she had any inkling of what he planned, he scooped her into his arms.

She didn't say a word. She felt so lethargic that she wasn't sure she could have moved on her own, and besides, being held close and carried felt good. Too soon she was being set gently down on one of the kitchen chairs.

Spencer proceeded to reheat the dinner she had made and serve it. He claimed it was delicious and she supposed it was, though she was distracted. She was struggling to put the pleasure she had just felt into a context that had to do with the baby.

She hadn't bargained for pleasure. She hadn't expected it, didn't *want* it. She didn't want to enjoy something enough to miss it when it was gone. After all, Spencer had done his job and was leaving the next day.

She knew he was aware of that, too, because what little conversation they had revolved around his manuscript, which would be ready with several more hours of work that night, and his plane, which was repaired and airworthy again. He was planning to fly to New York and drop the manuscript off, then continue south to Florida.

Because it seemed the only polite thing to do, she told him she would drive him to the airport. "It's only an hour," she pointed out when he frowned.

"I can take a cab."

"You could have taken a cab when you arrived, but you asked me to pick you up. So I can take you back." It was the least she could do, given how generous he'd been with his time.

Gruffly he said, "I thought we should talk then. There's no need for it now."

She knew that he was anxious to regain his freedom, and felt a twinge of hurt at the thought. But the hurt was good. It put a necessary wedge between them. Spencer had helped her with something she wanted, but that was where their involvement ended. The only thing left was to wind up their time together as cleanly as possible.

"I'm driving you," she said firmly.

"You have to work."

"I won't feel comfortable working until I know you're in the air."

"That eager to be rid of me, are you?"

She shot him a look of annoyance, and felt that annoyance all the way to her toes. She didn't know the answer to his question. Even aside from the sex, being with him hadn't been bad at all. It hadn't been as intimidating or anywhere near as awkward as she had thought it would be. But life had to go on, and that would mean reclaiming her office at home, stripping his bed of the sheets he had used and watching the calendar and her body for signs that what had happened in the dark of night between Spencer and her had worked.

They were in the Jaguar on their way to the airport Tuesday morning, with Jenna driving and Spencer brooding, when he asked her about that. "How soon will you know?"

She didn't equivocate. The baby was the only interest they had in each other now. "Thirteen days."

"I thought there were tests to tell you sooner."

"I don't trust them. If one said I was pregnant and it turned out I wasn't, I'd be devastated. I'd rather wait. If I'm a day late, I'll know. Then I can do the test to confirm it."

He was silent, staring out the side window. When they were within five minutes of the airport, he said, "I'll give you a call in two weeks to find out."

"I won't be here. I'll be in Hong Kong."

His head came around fast. "Hong Kong?" The silver in his blue eyes was alive, though whether from envy, curiosity or irritation she didn't know. "Why are you going to Hong Kong?"

"I'm touring the factories that make some of our things."

"*Alone?*"

She shook her head. "With a few of my people. We like to see things firsthand once or twice a year."

"You shouldn't be going now."

She pictured the front page of the newspaper as it had been that morning, and couldn't remember seeing Hong Kong listed among the world's current trouble spots. "Why not?"

His eyes flashed—quite definitely in irritation, she realized.

"Because you may be pregnant."

"If I am, what's happening inside me is so microscopic that going to Hong Kong won't affect it one way or another. Believe me," she said with a knowing chuckle and a protective hand on her stomach, "I would do *nothing* to endanger this child."

"I've done that trip many times. It's long and tiring. You don't call that a danger?"

"No. Neither does my doctor. Once I knew you'd help me, I asked him about it. He said that if an egg is going to be fertilized, it'll happen before I leave, and if it happens and is good, nothing about a trip like this can harm it."

"What if it isn't good? What if you have a miscarriage when you're halfway around the world?"

"A miscarriage at this stage is a period. I won't even know I was pregnant."

"What if you are, and you start getting morning sickness?"

"I won't. Morning sickness doesn't start until the fifth or sixth week at the earliest. If anything, this is the best time to go. If I'm here, I'll be looking at the calendar every day. If I'm there, I'll be distracted. The time will go faster." She took her eyes from the road long enough to see the doubt on his face. "Really, Spencer. It's not like I'm going there to party. Between the length of the

flight and the fact that this trip is strictly business, I'll
be getting plenty of sleep."

"*Will* you sleep on the flight?" he asked in such a way
that she was momentarily shaken. She hadn't thought
he would put two and two together where her emotions were concerned, but his tone was knowing
enough to suggest just that.

She kept her eyes peeled for the airport turnoff. "I always sleep on airplanes. That's the only way I can make
it through the flight. Actually, I've flown enough since
my parents died to be over the worst of the fear. The
statistics are in my favor. And Mom and Dad went
down in a small, private plane, while I only fly in the
largest commercial jets to be found."

"You'd love my plane," Spencer said tongue-in-
cheek, and looked out the window again.

Jenna wouldn't step foot in his plane for all the tea in
China, but that didn't mean she begrudged Spencer
flying it. She could understand the convenience, even
the pleasure. She could also understand that a person
might feel more in command with his own hands at the
controls, than with a stranger in charge. Personally, she
wanted size and bulk around her. It might be a delu-
sion, but she felt safer that way. She could also, with a
determined stretch of the imagination, pretend she was
simply sitting in a cabin-shaped transport moving
along the ground from point A to point B.

Feeling a gnawing in the pit of her stomach that she
was sure came from the dozens of small planes in sight,
she pulled up at Hangar C, turned off the engine and
launched into the speech she'd been preparing since
dawn. "Thank you, Spencer. I can't begin to tell you
how grateful I am for what you've done. You made the
time to be here, when you had a pile of your own work

to do, and I appreciate that. You were considerate and gentle. You made me feel less embarrassed than I might have. You were wonderful."

Slowly he turned to her, eyes piercing, jaw set. The look was intimidating. She wasn't sure what he was so angry about.

"I mean all that," she insisted.

"I'm sure you do."

"With any luck, I won't have to bother you again. I've already signed papers to the effect that I won't ask you for anything when it comes to this child. My lawyer has them. I'll have him send them to you by courier if that would make you feel better."

Spencer pushed the door open and climbed out. "What would make me feel better," he grumbled as he reached for his gear, "would be for you to stop thanking me as though I had just delivered a rush order of panty hose in time for your summer sale." He was leaning into the car, his eyes level with hers and narrowed. "What you and I did was fun. It was stimulating and satisfying. It was a nice diversion from my work." His voice sharpened. "And don't bother with a courier. I know where the papers are. When I need them, I'll get them." He straightened and slammed the door. Then he swung his duffel over his shoulder and walked off.

Jenna's eyes grew glassy. She blinked once, then again. She took a deep, shaky breath and let it out with a sigh, but she didn't move. She sat in the car until she saw Spencer come out of the hangar and approach one of the planes. It looked old and more battered than the rest. But his step didn't falter. He opened the door and threw his gear ahead of him before he climbed in. She saw him moving around the cockpit, then settling in behind the controls. After what seemed an eternity, the propellers started turning slowly, then faster. When they were little more than a round blur, the plane turned and headed away from the terminal. It advanced to the runway and paused. After a bit, it started forward again, gaining speed this time until, with a small bounce that made her gasp, it left the ground. She watched it gain altitude, watched it put distance between itself and her, watched until it was nothing but a speck in the sky.

Only then, with a vow to look nowhere but forward, did she start the car and head for work.

7

IN FACT, JENNA had grilled her doctor long and hard about the wisdom of going to Hong Kong. The trip had been planned six months earlier, when she hadn't known she'd be trying to make a baby. Knowing it now, she had been as skeptical as Spencer. But the doctor was right. If she was going to conceive that month, she would have conceived before takeoff. She would be flying first class, staying in a luxury hotel, eating in fine restaurants, taking taxis wherever she went. Anything that might happen under those conditions could just as easily happen at home, and for her peace of mind alone, she was better off busy than idle.

So, one week after Spencer flew south, she flew west, then west again, and to some extent she succeeded in not dwelling on whether there was a baby or not. From breakfast through dinner each day, she followed a comfortably busy schedule. Before breakfast, she prepared herself for those meetings; after dinner, she analyzed them. She only thought about the baby at night, when she was in bed awaiting sleep, and for the most part she was hopeful. During those times of doubt when she wished she had stayed home, where things were less eventful, she thought of the millions of unplanned pregnancies each year, of the women who went about their lives without realizing anything was amiss, who did things that were active, rigorous, even dangerous without losing their babies, and she was encouraged. Yes, she was active, but no more so than usual, and she didn't do anything that could even remotely be considered rigorous or dangerous.

Every morning, she took her temperature. From a low at the time of ovulation, it had risen to normal and was hovering there, which meant either that she would be getting her period or missing it.

She got it. Seven days into the trip, with three days to go before she flew home, she woke in the morning with proof that there wouldn't be a baby in April. The first thing she did was to burst into tears, but they didn't last long. She was too levelheaded to wallow in self-pity. After all, she and Spencer had only made love twice. Some couples tried for years before they succeeded. Hadn't her own doctor said it might take time? Hadn't he said she shouldn't be discouraged if she didn't immediately conceive?

They would try again. It was as simple as that.

Assuming Spencer was willing.

That thought haunted her through the final days of her trip. She found herself thinking about it not only at night, but when she was with other people, at meals and meetings. Spencer had been annoyed with her when he'd left. She assumed he had been feeling antsy after being stuck at her house for three full days. Granted he'd had to work on his book and probably would have been restless wherever he was, but he was at *her* house with *her*, so she took his restlessness personally.

He said he liked the sex. She wasn't sure she believed him, though she desperately wanted to. Sure, he climaxed, but for all she knew he was thinking of another woman when he did. It would be just like him to try to make her feel good. On the other hand, he had snapped when she'd mentioned the papers she'd signed, which told her that regardless of who was in his mind at the time, he liked the sex part more than the baby part.

Had the sex been good enough to bring him back for another round? It had been for her, good enough—terrific enough—for her to feel more than a shimmer of excitement at the thought of being with him again, but what did *she* know. Spencer was the most skilled man she'd ever been with. She seriously doubted the reverse was true, and if that was so, he had possibly moved on to another woman already.

She wanted him back. She wanted that baby. He was the only one who would do.

By the time she returned to Little Compton, she was dead tired. Ironically, that wouldn't have been so if she'd been pregnant. But between worrying about Spencer's reaction when she gave him the news, wondering about his willingness to try again and coping with her period, which took a toll on her strength in the best of times, she was washed out. Without bothering to phone either the office or her answering service, she went straight to bed. That was at five in the afternoon. By the time she got out of bed at nine the next morning, feeling far, far better than when she'd crawled in, she knew she owed Spencer an immediate call.

He wasn't home. Her answering service told her that he had tried her the day before. Her secretary at the office said the same thing. She tried him again, every hour on the hour, and with each unanswered call, she conjured up more disturbing reasons for his absence. All involved women.

Finally, at three that afternoon, he picked up the phone. Even before she spoke, he sounded hassled. "Yeah?"

"Spencer?"

There was a pause, then a tentative, "Is that you, Jenna?"

"Uh-huh."

"For *God's* sake, where have you been?" he thundered. "I thought you were due back yesterday. Did you decide you wanted an extra day in San Francisco, when you knew I was waiting to hear from you? That was a damned inconsiderate thing to do. There are phones in San Francisco. You could have called me from there." With barely a breath, he asked, "So are you, or aren't you?"

"I'm not," she said immediately. Clearly he was impatient to know if she was pregnant, though she didn't know whether he wanted her to be or not.

"You got your period?" His tone was calmer, but it gave nothing away.

"Right on time."

He was still for a minute. "Were you disappointed?"

"Very!" She thought that would be obvious. "I wanted the baby. And I didn't want to have to ask you to come up here again. I felt badly enough doing it the first time."

Cavalierly he said, "It wasn't any problem. I got the work done on my book, and I got my book to New York."

She wrapped the telephone cord around her hand. "Well, I'm glad of that, at least." She didn't know what else to say.

"Are you feeling okay?"

"A little jet-lagged, but one more night will fix that. Spencer, I didn't hang around San Francisco for an extra day. I had a two-hour layover at the airport and was

NO POSTAGE
NECESSARY
IF MAILED
IN THE
UNITED STATES

BUSINESS REPLY MAIL

FIRST CLASS MAIL   PERMIT NO. 717   BUFFALO, NY

POSTAGE WILL BE PAID BY ADDRESSEE

HARLEQUIN READER SERVICE
3010 WALDEN AVE
PO BOX 1867
BUFFALO NY 14240-9952

DETACH ALONG DOTTED LINE

on the first plane back here. By the time I got home, I was so tired I couldn't keep my head up."

"See? You shouldn't have gone in the first place. It was an exhausting trip."

"I felt great until I got my period," she said, but she didn't see the point of elaborating, so she turned the tables. "Besides, I've been trying to call you all day. If you were so anxious to hear from me, you should have stuck around."

He suddenly sounded tired himself. "I've been with my lawyers all day. The court is still holding us up on these exploration rights, and time's running out. We've been trying to negotiate a compromise settlement with the other party, but so far it's a no-go."

"He won't give in at all?"

"Oh, he'll give in, but not as much as I need him to, to make it worth my time and effort to do the salvaging."

"What happens now?"

He sighed. "We wait for the court to reach a decision."

"How much time do you have?"

"Before hurricane season sets in? A few weeks. Even if the court was to hand down its decision tomorrow, we wouldn't have much time. I guess I'll be waiting until November to begin."

"What will you do in the meantime?" she asked. She was thinking that if he had time on his hands, he wouldn't mind making another trip north.

"I'll do research. Maybe fly down to the Yucatán and see what's happening there, or visit friends in Michigan. I don't know. It's frustrating."

Since she didn't think she'd have a better opening, she took a breath and forged ahead. "Would you—do you think you'd be willing to come up here again?"

"You mean, to try for the baby? Sure. I told you I'd help you."

So easy! She felt a weight lift from her heart. "Ahh. I was worried you'd had enough the first time."

"I made a commitment. I'll see it through—not that I've had a change of heart about wanting a kid of mine running around, but if there has to be one, I'd rather have it be yours than someone else's."

Jenna felt a thickening in her throat. It was a minute before she was able to produce sound, and then it was a soft "Thank you. Thank you, Spencer. You'll never be sorry, I promise you that. This baby will be the most special, special child in the world."

"That could be good or bad. For the time being, why don't we concentrate on getting it conceived. When should I fly up?"

"Uh, ten days, I think."

"You *think?*" He clucked his tongue and said in a teasing tone, "You're slipping, Jenna. Usually you know exactly when, why and for how long."

She felt instantly sheepish. "I know, but I haven't been thinking beyond getting you to agree to try again. If you want to hold on, I'll get my calendar."

"No need to do that now. I'll call you in a few days."

"But you'll want to make plans."

"Yeah, so I don't have a conflict with all the high action that's taking place here."

He was being facetious, of course. She could hear that, along with a note of disgust in his voice, and it occurred to her that a diversionary trip back to Rhode Island might be just what he needed to relieve the tedium of waiting for the court's decision on the salvage rights to his galleon.

"By the way," he said, "how was Hong Kong?"

"It was great, really. Our meetings went well, and the tours were interesting. We visited several factories that we're not using now but may be able to use next year. Our lawyers will start negotiating come fall."

"Will you have go back there then?"

"No. I'll make another visit in the spring."

"What if you're pregnant by then?"

"I won't go."

"Are you sorry you did this time?"

She had been half expecting the question. He had been against the trip from the start, had said it would be too tiring, and he had reminded her of that moments earlier. She didn't think she heard an I-told-you-so now, still she said with conviction, "If you're asking whether I feel that the trip had something to do with my not being pregnant, the answer is no. I got my period right on time, and it's been no heavier than usual. It's not a spontaneous abortion, just a period. I wasn't pregnant, that's all. Maybe if we'd done this in the doctor's office—"

"That wouldn't have worked."

"How do you know?"

"I just know," he said lightly. "Listen, don't worry about it. It'll happen this time. I'll call you soon to find out the date. Take care, Jenna."

THE LIGHTNESS in Spencer's voice hadn't been for show. He was legitimately pleased to be seeing Jenna again. The timing was right; he had nothing better to do. She was easy to be with, and the sex had been great. The only thing that bugged him was when she started talk-

ing about signing papers. Hell, he trusted her. He didn't
for a minute believe that she would turn around and sue
him for child support, and even if she did, it wouldn't
be the end of the world. He had plenty of money. He
could easily establish a trust fund for the kid. In fact,
he'd probably do it, anyway. Then he wouldn't feel
guilty leading his own carefree life.

Great sex. He still couldn't believe it. Sure, he found
Jenna attractive, but he found lots of women attractive. That didn't mean that when he took them to bed
the world tipped and spun. It sure had with Jenna. He
didn't know why, since some of those other women
were more lush and sexy and *skilled* than her, but he
wasn't analyzing it too deeply. All that mattered was
that they were good in bed together.

Or good on the patio together.

Or good . . . where? He wondered where they'd do it
next. He liked variety. It added spice. Jenna found it
shocking, but that was part of the fun he had with her.
She came to sex expecting nothing. Each bit of pleasure she felt stunned her. She was nearly as naive as a
virgin, but there was a definite fire inside. His challenge was to draw it out.

That thought was foremost in his mind over the next
few days. He wanted Jenna to loosen up with him, but
he doubted she'd do that at home. Her life was too well
structured, her mind too tied into the idea of getting
pregnant. He wanted her to forget that, which meant,
for starters, changing the scenery. Yeah, he liked that
idea. When he let his imagination go, he could picture
all sorts of super things happening.

He was thinking of some of those things when he
called her later that week. Feeling buoyant, slightly

aroused and very masculine, he said, "Hi, angel. How're you doin'?"

Jenna hesitated. "Spencer?"

"Who else would be calling you 'angel'?"

"I didn't think *you* would. Are you—is everything all right?"

"Everything's fine. Still holding even, no word from the courts, but I'm doing okay. Did you figure out when you'll be needing me next?" He conjured an image of a stallion being brought to stud, and stood a little straighter.

"Uh-huh. I'll be ovulating again on August 5. That's a Monday. So I guess the Saturday before would be good, just like before."

"That's fine. How about meeting me in Washington?"

"Washington?"

"D.C. I have research to do at the Smithsonian." Research that could actually wait for another time, but would serve the same purpose as the work on his manuscript had. It gave them an out if being together got to be a drag. "You'd have time to shop or museum-hop or do whatever you want."

"There isn't much shopping I'd do."

"You can check out the competition, then. Can you take Monday and Tuesday off from work?"

"I can," she said hesitantly.

"Then do it. We'll have fun."

He heard her sigh. "Spencer, I don't know—"

"Want me to fly there and pick you up?"

"Oh, no," she said quickly, "that won't be necessary."

He chuckled. "You do know that you're safer flying with me than with a commercial pilot, don't you?"

She harrumphed. "That's what every private pilot says."

"Well, it's true—assuming the private pilot is worth his salt. The guy who flew your parents that day wasn't. He didn't check out the plane the way he was supposed to, and if he had, he would have found that leak. If he hadn't died himself, the FAA would have brought him up on charges. But not me. I check everything out, and I do it carefully. Believe me. I love myself too much to risk my life."

"Then I guess I can be confident you'll make it to Washington safely. As for me, there's a nice DC-9 flying there from Providence three times a day. I'll book two rooms at the Capital Hilton."

"No, you won't. I'm not staying in anything big and impersonal." Nor did he want two rooms. "Let me make the reservations. I'll call you next week to tell you where."

"I'm paying."

"You're not paying."

"Having a baby was my idea."

"Going to Washington was my idea."

"But the baby is the point of the trip."

"No, it's not. Super sex is."

"We're not going there for super sex."

"I sure am."

"Spencer." She fell silent. He could picture her blushing and felt an unexpected swell of affection for her.

"Jenna," he said gently, "don't worry about it, okay? You'll get your baby, and I'll get my super sex, and we'll both be happy as pigs in—"

"Spencer!"

"Sorry. But it's true. Talk with you next week, angel. Ciao."

SPENCER FLEW into Washington's National Airport at noon on Saturday, the third of August. After securing his plane in the private hangar, he went to the commercial terminal to wait for Jenna's arrival at one. When the big plane rolled up, he felt a pleasant sense of expectation. He found himself breaking into a grin when Jenna finally came through the door.

She looked pretty. Her dark hair was in a bun, but he could excuse that because of the heat. The rest of her—in a pair of linen walking shorts the color of apricots, a matching cotton blouse and flats—was so easy on the eye in a chic kind of way that he felt pride when she walked up to him and not someone else. But that wasn't what made him grin. What made him grin was her expression.

"You look," he said, taking the carryon from her shoulder, "like you can't decide whether to be relieved to be on the ground or terrified that you're here. Which is it?"

With a resigned twist of her lips, she said, "A little of both. My better judgment tells me we should be doing this back home."

"If we listened to your better judgment—" he put a light hand at her waist and started steering her through the crowd "—we'd have done it in the doctor's office, and just think of what we'd have missed."

She kept her eyes on where they were going.

He lowered his mouth to her ear. "No comment?"

"No comment."

Peering down into her face, he saw that she was blushing. He liked it when she did that. Blushing was a soft, feminine thing to do.

More important, though, she wasn't angry. And a "no comment" meant that she didn't disagree with him, which was an indirect acknowledgment of the pleasure she'd felt, which was a step in the right direction. By the time they were done making this baby of hers, he was determined to have her aware of the true joys of life.

He would go slow, however. That was half the fun. They had the weekend, plus Monday and part of Tuesday ahead of them. With a little luck, he might even convince her to stay longer, but he'd have to play that part by ear. He'd have to see if *he* wanted it. For all he knew, he'd be sick of her in two days, in which case he'd be the first one out of there on Tuesday morning.

But Tuesday morning was Tuesday morning. This was Saturday, and he had things planned. Jenna was still nervous about being with him—nowhere near as much as the previous month, but still nervous. So he intended to keep her busy. Well aside from his research, which he would tackle on Monday, there were things he wanted to do around the city. She could do them right along with him.

First, though, there was the hotel and a preliminary hurdle to be cleared. He had made reservations at Loweth Park, which was small and elegant and just right for a romantic interlude. Jenna must have sensed something of that when they entered the lobby, because she was crowding his elbow when the clerk passed over the reservation slip.

"Two rooms?" she whispered so that only Spencer could hear.

Concentrating on the paper before him, he whispered back, "A suite."

"Not a suite. Two separate rooms."

"The suite has two rooms." He took his wallet from his pants.

"Two bedrooms?"

"Waste of money."

"*Spencer.*"

"I'll take the couch." With a smile for the clerk, he flattened a charge card on the paper and passed both across the counter. In full voice, he asked, "This room has a king-size bed?" He managed not to laugh when Jenna made a small sound of dismay beside him.

"That's right, sir. Just as you requested."

Jenna left his side. When he had finished checking in, he found her sitting in one of the large wing chairs, looking regal in a vulnerable way. He cocked a brow in the direction the bellboy was taking their bags. Slowly she rose from the chair and rejoined him.

"This isn't right," she said quietly.

He took her arm and spoke softly as they walked toward the elevator. "Sure, it is. Given what we're here for, it didn't make sense to take separate rooms—or to take a two-bedroom suite. The bed is big enough so we can have our own sides, and I really will take the sofa, if you want." Not that he expected it would come to that. Her problem was that she thought too much. When she wasn't thinking—like the last time, on her patio, after she'd had such a sweet climax—she was pliant. If they had been in a bed then, he would have stayed the night, and she wouldn't have fought him on it.

So he had to drive her out of her mind with pleasure. That was all.

8

THE ROOM WAS BEAUTIFUL. It was colonial in style, lushly done in rich burgundies and greens. The bed was king-size, indeed, and covered in velvet, as were a chair and love seat in the bedroom and more chairs and a sofa in the sitting room.

Though Jenna didn't comment on the decor, Spencer watched her run a hand along the velvet, linger before the oil paintings, carefully set her makeup case on the marble dressing table. She was used to fine things, he knew; still, she appreciated them. He liked that. He also liked the way wisps of her hair had come free of its knot, and he didn't want her tucking them back in. So, telling her that they had lots to do, he quickly ushered her from the suite.

They spent the rest of the afternoon walking. Spencer hadn't planned it that way; he had thought Jenna would tire long before he did, but she kept pace with him, and contentedly so. Neither of them were strangers to the city, so it wasn't a matter of sight-seeing as much as catching the spirit of those around them who were visiting the city for the first time. They held hands as they walked, talked when the mood struck, smiled often. The day was sunny and warm enough to force regular stops for cold drinks, and that was fun, too. They hit all the tourist spots—the monuments and memorials, the Mall, Capitol Hill—and some out-of-the-way places that they both knew. Late in the afternoon, on impulse, they ducked into a theater to catch a movie neither of them had seen. By the time it was over, they were famished, so they stopped for dinner—all the way from appetizer to dessert—then were so stuffed that they had to walk more. It was after eleven when they finally returned to the hotel.

Spencer was all too aware of what they'd be doing once they reached their suite. He had spent the afternoon trying not to think about it and had succeeded simply because conversation with Jenna had been engrossing and diverting. But the movie had been a sexy one, and Jenna had looked so sweet sitting across from him in the restaurant that he waged a losing battle. Increasingly his mind had fast-forwarded. During those times, his hunger must have shown, because Jenna's cheeks had pinkened and her eyes grown evasive. She held his hand, though, during the walk back to the hotel and didn't let go when they passed through the lobby.

Once in the elevator, he tightened his grip. "You're not gonna get nervous on me, are you?"

She didn't pretend not to know what he meant. "Of course I am. I wouldn't be me if I didn't."

"I won't let you get away with it," he warned, and the instant they entered the suite, without switching on a light, he backed her to the door, caged her there with his body and took her face in his hands. "I'm kissing you this time."

She shook her head. "Don't."

He traced the corner of her mouth with his thumb. "Can you give me a good reason not to?"

She nodded. "We're not lovers."

"We sure as hell are." His thumb brushed her cheek.

"Not in the real sense. What we're doing is purely functional."

He shook his head and gave her more of his weight. "It ceased to be purely functional way back on your patio. Maybe even before that, but you won't admit it."

"I can't."

He slid the back of his finger along her jaw, which was soft and smooth and delicate. "Why not?"

"Because it ends with the conception of this baby."

It occurred to Spencer just then that it didn't have to, that they could remain lovers longer if they wanted. Then he thought of the complications, the *far-reaching* complications, but they couldn't possibly be sorted out when he had sex on his mind. So, rather than argue, he cupped her chin in his hand and held her still for his kiss.

She caught her breath at the first touch—that tiny sound of surprised pleasure she often made, which he loved—and flattened a hand on his chest, but she didn't push him away. Giving her time, he drew back, but only for the space of a breath. He had felt the same surprised pleasure she had and wanted more. He touched her lips again, stroking them lightly, gentling her.

At first, aside from the quickening of her breathing, she was still. She didn't move her mouth, didn't move her body. He imagined she wanted to stop him but couldn't work her way through the pleasure she felt to do it. So he kept the pleasure going—it was easy enough to do, his heat was rising—made his kisses progressively deep and long. He slid both hands into her hair and tipped her face higher. He teased her tongue with his, then withdrew and dragged his mouth over her cheeks to her eyes, which he kissed closed. The brush of her lashes teased him, so whisper light against his skin that he began to shake with a greater need. Her lips were open when he returned to them, and with his hungry reclaiming, he felt her first, tentative response.

That response, so new and shy and sweet, brought him to near-full arousal. "Ahh, angel," he moaned against her hair, and lifted her into his arms. He carried her into the bedroom and pulled back the spread, then set her on the sheets.

She sat right up. "I . . . the bathroom."

"No," he whispered. Bracing himself on a knee, he caught her mouth and held it in a suctioning grip while he started unbuttoning his shirt.

"I want," she managed breathlessly, "my nightgown."

Tossing the shirt aside, he buried his face against her neck. "No, angel. I want to feel you."

But she slid out from under him, and was halfway across the room before he could reach her. Telling himself that there would be other times when she would be naked for him, he got rid of the rest of his clothes. He was waiting at the door to sweep her up again, nightgown and all, when she left the bathroom.

"So macho," she whispered.

But her arms were around his neck, and if she minded his gesture, she didn't let on. Nor did she object when his mouth covered hers before she hit the sheets, or when he made an immediate place for himself between her legs, or when he filled that part of that space with his hand and brought her to a heated climax. Her insides were still pulsing when he entered her, and if the white nightgown was any obstacle to pleasure, Spencer would have been hard put to say it, because, in exchange for leaving the garment on, she began moving her hands on his body. She had never participated quite that way before. Her touch was light and shy, with such devastating effect that his own climax came nearly as quickly and every bit as powerfully as hers had.

Then she slept in his arms as though it was the most natural thing in the world to do, as though there had never been talk of separate bedrooms or separate sides of a king-size bed or, heaven help them, his using the sofa. True, when she awoke to daylight the next morning, she slid away, but he understood that. Relatively speaking, she had come a long way. If he was patient, she would come another long way yet. And he could be patient. For a treasure, he had all the patience in the world.

JENNA KNEW she was falling in love with Spencer. The knowledge hit her hard on Sunday morning when, after a late brunch in bed, he rented a car and drove them to visit friends of his in Virginia. Sitting in the passenger's seat for a two-hour blend of easy conversation and companionable silence, she had time to reflect on the previous day. She'd had a wonderful time with him— she couldn't deny it—and that included what they'd done in bed. Yes, what they'd done in bed. As a lover, Spencer was masterful. He had her wanting him the way she had never wanted another man, and it kept getting better and better. The wanting was with her even now. No matter that they were in bucket seats, separated by a storage bin and the gearshift, she felt his presence as though they were still in bed, nestled against each other, sleeping—or pretending to. *He* had been sleeping; she had heard the evenness of his heartbeat by her ear; but she had found something so pleasurable in lying with him that she hadn't wanted to miss it by sleeping for long.

Vividly she remembered the softness of his chest hair against her cheek, his clean scent, the firmness of his torso against hers, the length of the arm that circled her and held her in place. She remembered the way her leg had curved naturally over his, and the way he had slept with his face buried in her hair.

Oh, yes, she was falling in love. Try as she might to find things to hate about Spencer, she couldn't. She supposed she could take that as a tribute to her own judgment, that the man she had chosen to father her child was as close to perfect as a man could be. But it didn't bode well for her future, in which Spencer had no role at all.

So what was she to do? Was she to go back to pushing him away and trying to keep their lovemaking as uninvolved as possible? That made sense. At least if she could keep reminding herself of the reason they were together, she had a chance of keeping her feelings for him within bounds. The problem was that when she was with him, when they were doing things together, she had trouble thinking straight.

It was a good thing she didn't have to remember to use birth control, she mused. She'd be pregnant for sure then.

"What is it?" he asked, darting her short, repeated glances.

"What?"

"You chuckled."

She hadn't realized it. Blushing but unable to help it, she said, "It was nothing. A Murphy's Law kind of thing."

He reached over and took her hand. She liked it when he did that. His hand was large and strong, and made her feel protected. This time he anchored it to his thigh—clad in jeans today—and held it until they turned in at his friends' farm.

Jenna liked his friends. Spencer had gone to school years earlier with the female half of the couple, and he and the male half had subsequently become friends. The couple raised horses. Jenna, who had always wished Rhode Island were lush enough for that, loved seeing the stables, the paddock, the pastures. Though she had never ridden a horse previously, she was eager to try—then proud when she held her own on the albeit gentle mount they gave her. Spencer stayed by her side for all but the brief periods of time when he gave his own horse free rein. She didn't begrudge him those times. He needed the freedom himself, and besides, he was a heart-stopping sight on a horse.

It was dark before they left Virginia. Having slept only intermittently the previous night, Jenna managed to stay awake during the drive back, but she was in bed and sound asleep by the time Spencer returned after disposing of the car. She woke up several times during the night to an awareness of the warmth of his body beside her and, selfishly, didn't fight its pull. He would be gone soon enough, she knew, but before he left, she wanted the closeness he was so willing to offer. Somehow that didn't seem wrong.

So she curled against him in defiance of the fact that he was Caroline's brother, that he was a world-renowned adventurer and author, that he would be back to his own life before long. If nothing else, she reasoned, he would know that his baby's mother was a woman worthy of warmth and affection.

SPENCER WAS IN PAIN. The last thing he wanted to do was to climb out of bed on Monday morning, and it didn't have to do with the soreness of his thighs, but rather what lay hard and heavy between them. Morning desire had always been a problem for him, but waking up to a snuggling Jenna made the problem ten times worse. He shifted her in his arms and rubbed his lips against her forehead, then lay for a while wondering how much more he dared do. She wasn't a daylight lover. He would make her one yet, but he couldn't rush her. She was still thinking of the baby, and had her mind set on the night.

The night. *That* night. He wasn't sure if he could wait. Closing his eyes, he took a tortured breath.

"Spencer?" came a whisper from his chest.

"Umm?" He was afraid to say much, lest she move away.

"Are you okay?"

"Just fine."

"You sound uncomfortable." Before he could explain that the discomfort was a sweet agony, she rolled out of his arms and sat up on her side of the bed. Her hair was a tangle around her head. She pushed it back with a hand, sat that way for a minute, then freed herself of the sheet and swung her legs to the floor.

In her innocent white gown, with her slenderness apparent and her hair a dark, seductive cloud, she looked as exotic as the most delicate of South Seas beauties. Spencer would have given his right arm to lunge for her and drag her back to bed.

In a moment of pique that was directed as much at his own damnable self-control as at her, he said, "I wasn't just uncomfortable. I was—am—in excruciating pain."

She looked back at him in alarm, but the alarm faded when she caught sight of the shape of the sheet. "Oh," she said, and blushed.

He laughed in spite of himself and rolled away. "I would suggest," he called over a shoulder, "that we get dressed and out of here fast. Anything else, and I can't promise I'll behave." The next thing he heard was the soft click of the bathroom door.

Fifteen minutes later, she emerged fully dressed and ready to let him take his turn, and that, too, was torture. The bathroom was filled with the lingering warmth from her shower and the scent of her body lotion. He had to run the water at its coldest and stand under it for a bone-numbing ten minutes before he was finally under control.

They ate breakfast in the hotel dining room. Then Spencer set out for the Smithsonian. He asked Jenna if she wanted to come, but she was intent on museum-hopping, and it was just as well. He needed a break. She was a temptation to look at. He prayed that out of sight would be out of mind.

For the most part, it was. He spent the day poring through ancient records of vessels that had sailed at the time of his Spanish galleon. He traced their routes on yellowed maps and made notes of their cargo, as recorded in crude journals that demanded his close attention. There was referencing and cross-referencing to be done, papers of earlier researchers to study, and he found it all as intriguing as he'd known it would be. Then the mustiness of the air got to him. His mind slowed and started to wander. He felt not so much bored as drained of energy.

The office he was using was in the basement of one of the lesser buildings of the Smithsonian, and wasn't far from where the records he needed were stored. He had given Jenna the number of the room and told her that he would be there at least until six, and that if she finished early and wanted to join him, she could. By midafternoon, he was listening for her footsteps in the hall.

Shortly before six, he heard them. When she knocked on the door and poked her head in, he felt a return of the energy he had been lacking. He also felt a return of the desire, which, in his enervated state, hit him all the harder. Hoping action would diffuse it, he rose from the desk and quickly gathered together the books he'd been using.

"I'll wait if you want to work more," Jenna said, but he simply handed her a book to carry.

"I've had enough." He pushed his notes into a pile and put them in his briefcase. "If I were superstitious, I wouldn't be touching these records. The court still has to rule in my favor." He put the books on top of his briefcase and lifted the lot. "Let's get these returned." He shut off the light, locked the door and started down the hall. "How was your day?"

"Fun."

"Which museums did you hit?"

"The Portrait Gallery and the Hirschorn. I had lunch on the terrace at the Botanic Garden."

"You went to the Botanic Garden without me?" The Botanic Garden was his favorite. Being there was the next best thing to being on a tropical island.

She smiled him an apology. "Sorry. But I couldn't resist. I love that place."

"You should've saved it. You should've gone shopping, instead. That's what most women would have done." His words were gruff, offered in jest, but they

made him think. Jenna wasn't like other women. He
was just coming to realize that. She didn't follow a
crowd, didn't cling to tradition for its own sake, didn't
run from new experiences. She had walked all over
Washington with him, had ducked into a movie theater on the spur of the moment, had bravely climbed up
on that horse. She had decided that she wanted a baby,
so she'd set out to get one. He respected that.

Now she sent him a chiding look, but it was no
harsher than his tone had been, and he was struck once
again by how pretty—no, how beautiful she was with
her dark hair and her pale skin, how sweet and innocent, how sexy.

"Here we go," he said in a thick voice, and separated
a key from the others. After using it, he shouldered
open a door that took them out of the dimly lit hall and
into a pitch-black storage room. He hit a switch with
his elbow to give them light, dropped his briefcase on
a table by the door, took his books and Jenna's and returned them to the shelves from which he'd removed
them several hours earlier.

Jenna was leaning against the table by his briefcase.
Her eyes smiled when he emerged from the stacks, and
he felt a little flip-flop inside. From nowhere came a
naughty thought. Actually it wasn't from nowhere;
he'd been thinking naughty thoughts all his life. This
one, though, he immediately pushed from mind. Jenna
wasn't the type.

Then he remembered what he'd been thinking about
her, that she wasn't any "type," and the naughty
thought returned.

Pushing at the light switch, he plunged them into
darkness, but it was Jenna he reached for, not the door.
"I missed you today," he said, and brought her close.

"Did you miss me, too?" His head was already descending, and before she could answer, he covered her mouth with his.

It was supposed to be a mischievous kiss, stolen in the black belly of the Smithsonian, but within seconds, it erupted with the hunger he had been feeling so strongly that morning. She tasted faintly of coffee and smelled of rare flowers, both of which pleased him, but it was the stealth of her arms winding around his neck that pleased him most of all.

He kissed her deeply, using his tongue to its utmost, but that wasn't enough. He caressed her back, brought his hands forward and caressed her breasts, but that wasn't enough, either. So he bent his head to her neck and planted wet kisses down that slender column to where the slim strap of her sun dress lay on her shoulder.

Her arms were coiled around his neck. Taking encouragement from that, he reached behind her and unzipped her dress.

"Spence?" she whispered breathlessly.

He unhooked her bra and reached for her hands. "If I don't feel you, I'll die." Pulling her hands down, he drew the dress and bra from her breasts.

"Here?" she cried, then cried again when he took her warm flesh in his palms.

"Oh, yeah, here." He felt her swell and wished he could see her. Since he couldn't, he lowered his head.

"Someone could walk in—" She caught her breath sharply when he opened his mouth on her breast. She said his name again, pleadingly this time, and while he was waiting for her to push him away, she surprised him by fastening her fingers in his hair.

He drew her into his mouth, nipped her softly with his teeth, used his tongue to make her wet. His thumb rolled over that wetness while he moved to the other breast, and when it was as wet, he left both hands on her and rose to her mouth. For the first time, her kiss was as open, as deep, as hungry as his was.

Needing her more badly than he'd have imagined possible, he dragged his mouth away. "Help me," he whispered, and pulled up her dress.

"Are you sure we can do this?" she whispered back, but her hands helped his.

"The only thing I'm sure of," he said as he opened his pants, "is that we can't *not* do it."

She clutched his bare hips. "What if someone comes along?"

"I'll take that risk." He splayed his hands over her bottom and lifted her onto the table. When he felt her legs circle him, he captured her mouth and thrust into her.

He would never get over how tight she was, or how delicate, or how sweet smelling, or how right. She was made for him. Their fit was ideal. Again and again, he buried himself in her, only to withdraw for the sake of stroking the warm, wet walls that hugged him. He was thinking that nothing could be better when she started to come apart in his arms. Her first small cry sent him into a shattering orgasm.

Afterward, she was the first to speak. "My God, I don't believe this." There was, indeed, disbelief in her voice, but delight as well.

He was still breathing heavily. "The room?"

"Room, table, building—" She paused and in a smaller voice said, "That was the first time I've ever climaxed during intercourse."

He suspected she wouldn't have confessed in the light, and he knew the feeling. In a voice that wasn't so much small as humble and the tiniest bit awed, he said, "Do you know how rare it is for two people to come at the same time?"

She drew her head away from his shoulder. "Is it?"

"Yes. It's only happened to me once before in my life."

"I don't believe you."

"So help me God, it's true."

"But you're so *experienced*."

"Yeah, well, not in the kind of thing we just shared." And that included the one other time he had climaxed at the same time as his lover. That time had been purely accidental. This time there had been deep emotions involved.

He stroked her legs all the way around to her ankles, then reluctantly eased them from his hips. "I guess we blew the missionary position, huh?"

"Guess so," she murmured. He could tell by the small, slithering sounds that she was putting on her bra.

"Are you gonna hate me in the morning for this?"

"Of course not."

He pulled up his pants. "Do we get to do it again tonight?"

"I don't know. We shouldn't."

"Because I won't be at full potency? Somehow I don't think that's an issue here, and it's got nothing to do with ego." He zipped up. "You have a powerful effect on me, Jenna."

The sounds that had been telling him she was putting her dress back in place suddenly stopped. Hesitantly she asked, "Is that really true?"

"Can't you tell?"

"Words are words. A person can say what he or she thinks the other wants to hear. It's done a lot."

Annoyed that her earlier experience with men had been so deflating, he snapped, "Not by me." He gentled his tone. "And besides, it isn't only the words. It's the action that goes with them. Do you think I could make love to you the way I do if my attraction to you wasn't potent? And with nearly no foreplay!"

Jenna was quiet.

"Well?" he prodded.

"Okay."

"Okay, we can do it again tonight?"

"Okay, you're attracted to me."

He sighed. "Such enthusiasm."

She went back to dressing. "I'm pleased."

"Such *enthusiasm*."

It was her turn to sigh. "Enthusiasm can be a dangerous thing. We're leaving tomorrow."

"We don't have to," he said because it seemed like the time. "I'm pretty free right about now."

"I'm not. I have McCue's."

"And you're the boss." He ran his hands up her arms to her shoulders. "You're not punching a time clock." He reached behind to raise her zipper. "You can take another day off if you want." He barely had to move to put his mouth to her temple. "Do it, angel. Spend another day with me."

"Oh, Spencer," she whispered, and slipped her arms around his waist.

Once upon a time, Spencer would have heard that whisper and felt those arms, and turned and run in the opposite direction as fast and as far as he could. No woman had ever tied him down. He had never allowed or wanted one to. And he wasn't sure he did now. All he knew was that the sound of his name, whispered so sweetly by Jenna, made his heart swell, while the feel of her arms warmed something he hadn't realized was cold, until now.

What he felt was confusing. He and Jenna didn't have a future. Not in the long run. He had his travels; she had McCue's. And then there was the matter of the baby. She was vehement in her determination to raise it alone, and that was fine, because he didn't want to change diapers.

But, damn it, he liked being with Jenna.

"Stay," he whispered. "Just for the fun of it. One more day. I'll be a good boy and get on top, and I'll make sure you don't move for an hour afterward. I'll even do it in that bed again, though it goes against my better judgment to make love in the same place twice."

She growled in frustration. "Ugh, Spencer, you're impossible."

"But irresistible. Will you stay?"

"I'll stay."

"Until Wednesday morning?"

"Until Wednesday morning, but I *have* to leave then, and I mean it, Spencer. I have a board meeting on Thursday morning. I'm the chairman. I can't miss it."

"You won't." He tipped up her chin and planted a smacking kiss on her mouth. "Thank you, Jenna. You won't regret this."

JENNA DIDN'T, though if Spencer had told her what he'd intended, she might have had second thoughts.

He didn't make love to her on Monday night, which threw her off balance partly because she wanted him to. Rather, he came up with tickets to see the Kirov Ballet at Wolf Trap Farm, and hired a limousine to take them there. It occurred to her that he might try something risqué in the long back seat on the way home, but he didn't, and once in the hotel room, he settled her comfortably against him to watch a late movie that he swore was classic horror. Never a horror fan, she fell asleep as soon as she realized that he fully intended to watch.

She woke up in his arms on Tuesday morning. He shifted her against him. He stroked her back and kissed her softly. She knew he was aroused, could feel it in his body, yet he made no move to make love. Instead, in a lazy voice, he told her about his place in the Keys and what it was like to wake up to the sun spilling across the ocean.

"I know what it's like," she told him. "I see it, too."

"But you're up north where it's cold. In my neck of the woods, you can walk stark naked on the deck just about year-round."

"God help the neighbors."

"No neighbors close enough to care. Kind of like your patio. Only warmer."

That said, he climbed out of bed. He was naked—he always slept naked—and though she saw only his back as he went into the bathroom, that was enough. His hips were narrow, his buttocks tight. Both made his shoulders look all the broader. His back and legs were tanned a dark bronze. His walk was smooth and fluid.

Jenna had seen many a male model in her line of work, and while some had been younger and more handsome, none could hold a candle to Spencer for sheer virility.

When he emerged from the bathroom moments later, he was wearing a robe, but she couldn't forget what he looked like without it. The image haunted her, stirring her blood each time she gave in to it, which was often.

She didn't have anything—like work—to divert her mind. And Spencer was there, never farther from her than a yell.

They had breakfast in the room. While he showered, she called her secretary to say that she wouldn't be back until the next day. Then she took her turn in the shower. When she was done, they set out for Georgetown.

Had it not been for the ache inside her, the day would have been as carefree as the others had been. But alongside that image of a naked Spencer was one of his small plane heading south in the morning. If she was pregnant, there wouldn't be any excuse for their meeting again. He might be attracted to her, but he didn't want anything to do with a baby, and she still wanted the baby—now more than ever. While Spencer chased after his adventures, she would have his baby to love.

But he wasn't gone yet. She was reminded of that time and time again—when he caught her hand in his, when he grinned at her, when he turned his blue eyes on her in a way that promised good things to come. He seemed oblivious to the women who looked at him, who were drawn either by those eyes or his height or his scar. He made Jenna feel as though she were the only one worthy of notice. No man had ever made her feel that way, which was why, by the time they'd had dinner that night and lingered over a third cup of coffee, Jenna was ready to follow him to the ends of the earth. When he asked if she wanted to go back to the room, she didn't trust herself to do anything but nod.

The hotel was quiet. They took the elevator to their floor and walked down the hall. Spencer unlocked the door and followed her in. Then, coming up behind, he wrapped her in his arms.

"Jenna?"

She closed her eyes and leaned back against him. "Yes?"

"I want you."

That much was becoming clearer by the minute, to her infinite relief. "You could have had me last night."

"I know. But I wanted to wait. I wanted you to feel the wanting, too."

Softly, clasping his wrist, she said, "I do."

"Will you do something for me, then?"

"That depends what it is."

"I want you to leave the nightgown in the bathroom. I won't put the light on, if that'll make it easier, but I want to feel all of you against me."

Two days earlier, Jenna might have balked, but two days earlier she hadn't known this awful wanting. Shyness was just fine, until it interfered with satisfaction, and satisfaction was what she needed from Spencer. He was her lover, yes, *her lover*. She couldn't deny it any longer. He wanted her naked against him. She wanted it, too.

"Okay," she said softly, and heard him drag in a rough breath.

"You will?"

"Yes."

Turning her in his arms, he kissed her with a tenderness that might have brought tears to her eyes if she hadn't been burning inside, burning inside already. That was what he did to her.

She was hanging on to the lapels of his shirt when he released her mouth. "Will you undress, too?" she whispered.

"I always do."

"But when I do? At the same time?"

"If you want."

"I do."

He gave her another, even softer kiss, then began to unbutton his shirt. She stepped out of her flats and unfastened her belt. When it was discarded, she unzipped her walking shorts and slipped them off. Spencer was unfastening his pants, but his eyes were on her, and though the room was dark, she imagined those blue eyes saw everything. Once she would have found that daunting, and she still half expected a wave of modesty to hit, but it didn't. The night was a veil of emotion, telling her that what she was doing was right. So she drew her shirt over her head and dropped it, then did the same with her bra and panties. When she looked at Spencer, he was standing in the shadows, as straight and naked as she.

"Come here," he said quietly.

Her feet made no noise on the carpet. Heart pounding, she stood before him, half wishing she could see more of him, half grateful she couldn't. When he still didn't move, she touched his chest. "Spence?"

His voice was low when he said, "That's what I want. Touch me more, angel. Your hand feels like heaven."

For a minute, she didn't do anything. She had never been much of an activist where sex was concerned. But touching Spencer seemed as natural now as holding his hand had been earlier. It was satisfying in ways she hadn't expected. And stimulating.

Her hand trembled over his chest. She shaped her palm to his shoulder, and when the fit felt incredibly good, let the other palm do the same. His skin was smooth there. Seeking more texture, she dragged her hands down his hair-roughened chest, touching nipples that were tiny and tight. His breathing grew more

ragged, but that goaded her on. Lightly her fingertips
followed the wedge of dark hair that tapered into a thin
line down his middle. She flattened her palms on his
waist and slid them down his flanks, then to the front
of his thighs.

He whispered her name in a sound of sheer pain. Her
hands froze; her eyes flew to his. While she tried to read
his feelings, he made another, more strangled sound.
"Don't stop, angel. Don't stop now. Keep going. I need
you to touch me there, too."

Jenna would have laughed in relief if she hadn't been
so curious. She touched him where he had asked. He
was stretched into silk—she was amazed at how sleek,
and how hard, how erect. She explored him with one
hand, then with both until his groan reminded her that
the rest of him was still waiting. Slipping her arms
around him, she came against him naked for the very
first time.

That full-body touch was his undoing. Whatever re-
straint he'd had was suddenly gone. He kissed her and
touched her like a man who couldn't get enough of either. He brought her to one climax before, then another when he was inside her, and after he had come
himself, he stayed with her only until he had recovered
his breath. Then, albeit careful to keep her on her back,
he started all over again. This time, he kissed her ev-
erywhere. His mouth learned her body by inches, si-
lencing the few protests she made without a word.
Jenna was so stunned that anything could feel so good
for so long, that she soon ceased protesting anything.
She trusted that Spencer knew what he was doing, and
put herself into his care.

She lost count of how many times they made love.
She ceased to care about who was on top, how long she

lay still afterward or whether Spencer's sperm count was depleted.

She didn't exactly feel a spark. In fact, by the time morning came, she was so pleasantly numb that she wasn't sure she would have felt a full-fledged explosion if it happened inside. But she knew. *She knew.* At some point that night, they had made a baby. All that was left was to wait two weeks for the proof.

9

SURE ENOUGH, Jenna didn't get her period on the day the calendar said she was due. She didn't feel bloated or achy, the way she normally did at that time of the month. And her home pregnancy test read positive.

She was elated. Secret smiles came often and lingered. She had badly wanted a baby; now she would have one. And *what* a baby. Spencer's child would be outstanding. She couldn't wait to feel it inside her, to see it, to hold it. A May baby. Nine months seemed an eternity to wait.

That night, standing unclothed at the bathroom mirror, she looked closely at her body. Nothing of the pregnancy showed. Her breasts were no fuller than before, her stomach just as flat. She assumed it would be several more weeks before she detected the first of the changes.

Later, lying in bed with the same soft smile that had been coming and going all day, she thought about that. She wasn't in a rush to look pregnant. All along, she had intended to keep early word of the pregnancy private, simply because it was her own sweet secret and to be savored as such. She had envisioned waiting to tell her board of directors about the baby until the second trimester, and then only when she started to show. Some would disapprove of her choice of single motherhood, but by then she would be far enough along— and have enough plans made—to still their worries.

So, the board could wait to hear the news. And Jenna's friends could wait. Even Caroline could wait. But Spencer? He was the one she agonized over long into the night. He had called her the week before to see how she was doing—it was the highlight of her week—and had asked when her period was due. She had upped the date by a day, thinking that she wanted to be sure, *really* sure, before she told him she was pregnant.

Now she wasn't sure she wanted to tell him. She didn't want to give him the chance to say goodbye and never call again. She wanted another weekend with him. Just one more.

Was there harm in it? One little white lie? Not even a lie, but the failure to tell the whole truth? Was it so wrong, given how good he made her feel as a woman and how little of that feeling she'd had in her life? She was prepared to put being a mother above everything else, but before she did, would one last passionate fling be so awful?

She didn't think so, which was why, when he called her the following evening, she chose her words with care.

"Did you get it?" he asked after little more than a hello.

He didn't mince words, which was one of the things she loved about Spencer. He didn't hem and haw and beat around the bush like some of the men she knew. He had guts.

She hesitated just long enough to suggest pain, then spoke in a voice low enough to suggest apology. "I think we'll have to try again." She didn't elaborate. Understatement was better, silence even better than that.

"Ahh, angel, I'm sorry. Are you feeling lousy?"

"Not too bad."

"God, I'm sorry. I thought for sure something would have happened in Washington. I mean, we did it so much, and we were both so loose. What do you think the problem is?"

"I'm not sure there's any problem," she said firmly. She didn't want him worrying that there was something wrong with *him*. "Two months is nothing, really."

"I can't believe it's the position we use. I've been on top of you as much as under—and I refuse to believe it's because we did it too much—and don't even think that it might have worked if we'd done it in the doctor's office, because it wouldn't have. And even if it *might* have," he tacked on vehemently, "I wouldn't have missed the fun we had. It was good between us."

She felt the womanly parts of her coming alive. "I know."

"So we'll try again."

Softly she said, "If you don't mind."

"I don't mind." He sounded sober, but in no way put out.

"Thank you, Spencer. You're a good sport."

"Uh-huh. Yeah. Well, I have a new idea this time. If we were to follow past pattern, we'd be getting together in another two weeks. I think we ought to meet sooner, like in ten days, and I think you should plan to take a real vacation from work then. I have to be in New York right around that time. I could swing by and pick you up, then fly you down here. My place is perfect for a vacation."

"Your place?" She conjured up images of sunshine, seclusion and sand.

"It's warm and open. And relaxing. If there was ever a place to conceive a baby, this is it."

Jenna had no doubt that was true, though conception wasn't any longer a worry. The worry was her peace of mind. Seeing his home would make things harder when she had to forget him. Then again, she did want to see where he lived. "I suppose I could take a few days off," she conceded.

"Not a few days. I'm talking a real vacation."

She thought of the office and her appointment book for the next few weeks. The timing was actually fine. The end of August was the quietest time of the year. "I could take five days and a weekend," she suggested.

"I was thinking ten. Plus weekends. Two full weeks."

"I couldn't do that."

"Sure you could. Don't tell me much of anything gets done the week before or after Labor Day."

He had a point, she knew. "But I'm never gone from the office that long unless it's for business."

He paused for a minute before saying, "You'll be out longer than that when you have the baby."

"True, but I'll be close by and accessible by phone."

"Hey, I'm not talking a trip across the Sahara by camel. I'm talking the Florida Keys. We're civilized down here. We do have phones. If you were needed, someone could call. Come on, angel," he urged gently, "go for it."

He was right—about Labor Day, the phone, civilization—and she wanted to be with him. Thinking about it, she realized that she couldn't have asked for a better time or a nicer place. "Okay," she said. "But I'll meet you there. I can take a commercial flight into Miami, rent a car and drive down."

"I'll be in New York anyway. I want to fly you back."

"Your plane is too small."

"But it's my plane. I know it like the back of my hand. If there's anything wrong, I can sense it before it even shows up on the dials."

"Uh-huh. Seems to me you've had trouble with it in recent weeks."

"And the trouble was fixed well before I crashed."

"Obviously. If you'd crashed, you wouldn't be around to talk about it. Survival would have been impossible. That plane won't protect you from *anything*. I've seen it. It looks like it's held together by rubber bands."

"Rubber bands or not, in the past fifteen years I've criss-crossed this continent in that plane more times than you and I have fingers and toes combined. *Double* that. It's a safe plane, Jenna, and I'm a safe pilot."

"You may be, but I'm a basket case of a flyer. I'd drive you nuts before we ever got off the ground. Seriously, Spencer. It would be better for both of us if I just met you there."

He was quiet for a minute. Then, sounding surprisingly dejected, he said, "You don't trust me."

"I do. It's the plane I don't trust, and the weather."

Somberly he said, "I don't fly if either of those things are in question, which is more than I can say for the average commercial pilot. He has a schedule to keep. I don't. Do you honestly think I have a death wish?"

"Some people might think that, given the adventures you've had."

"But do you?"

After no more than a single heartbeat, she said, "No." He respected life. She could tell that from his books, and from everything she'd experienced with him.

"Then fly with me."

She squeezed her eyes shut. "Spencer, I'll be *so nervous.*"

"No, you won't, because you'll be sitting right beside me watching what I do, and you'll know that I wouldn't do anything to endanger either you or the baby that may be someday—if we can do it right this time." ·

She didn't want to fly on his plane. She *really* didn't want to. But she felt guilty letting him think there was no baby yet, when there was, and if it was an issue of trust, there was no one she trusted more than Spencer.

"You'll be sorry," she warned. "I'll be the worst passenger you've ever had. I may even get sick and throw up all over your cabin." A brainstorm! She was covered in the event of morning sickness!

His tone picked up. "No sweat. I'll bring barf bags. Hey, this is great, Jenna. We'll have a terrific time. I'm really looking forward to it."

"Uh-huh. Well, I will, too, once we get there. What should I bring?"

Based on the answer he gave—a bathing suit, shorts and T-shirts and a sun dress—Jenna surmised that life on Spencer's Key was thoroughly informal. Not that she expected or wanted anything different. Clothes were irrelevant. Being with Spencer was what mattered.

HE SENT HER FLOWERS, a dozen bright yellow roses. They arrived at her office early the next morning with a note that said, "Cheer up. The best things often take the most work. We'll make it this time. S." It was such a sweet, unnecessary thing to do—and made her feel so guilty—that she promptly burst into tears. She was abundantly grateful that she had beat most of her staff to work. She was the president of the company. Her people would be shocked to see her crying over a vase of roses.

But the roses stood proudly on her desk, giving her a tiny thrill each time she looked at them. When Spencer called two nights later, she thanked him profusely and assured him that the flowers had made her feel better. He called two nights after that to see if she was feeling all right, then three nights after that to make sure she hadn't had any trouble making vacation arrangements at the office, then, again, from New York the night before he picked her up, to make certain she was ready.

On the one hand, Jenna loved talking with him. On the other, she felt like a heel for deceiving him. So she decided that she would look her absolute spectacular best while she was with him. To that end, she had her hair conditioned and trimmed, had a facial, had a manicure and pedicure. Being a McCue, she also shopped. She visited five of her stores, scattered in three different states. All five were already filled with fall clothes, but each had fitness departments that were stocked with things like bathing suits, shorts and T-shirts year-round. She struck out when it came to a sun dress, but she had enough of her own not to mind. Moreover, several of the T-shirts she bought were oversized enough to be belted into dresses this trip, then worn loose later, when she needed more room.

She had one large suitcase and a well-stuffed carryon waiting when Spencer picked her up at the house. "All for a bathing suit, a couple of T-shirts and shorts and a sun dress?" he asked, eyeing the bags in dismay.

She didn't take offense. He was such a wonderful sight that she doubted she could have held much of anything against him—except the plane, which she was making a monumental effort to forget. "I knew how hot it would be down there and that I'd be sweating a lot. I wanted to have fresh clothes to change into."

"I could keep you naked. It'd be simpler." His eyes teased her with something indecent, and in spite of all they had shared, she felt a blush warm her cheeks. He laughed at that and picked up her bags. "Let's go."

She was fine on the way to the airstrip. She didn't allow herself to think that this flight would be any different from the others she'd taken. Her heart rose to her throat when she spotted the plane, but she pushed it back down. People flew on small planes every day, she told herself. She looked out over the other private planes that were moving in the area of the runway. She didn't expect any of those to crash. There was no reason for her to believe Spencer's would.

It struck her then that she was responsible not only for her own life, but for the baby's, too, and she felt a sudden need to tell Spencer that. But if she told him about the baby, he wouldn't feel impelled to take her anywhere, and she wanted so to be with him. Besides, when all was said and done, she trusted him with her life.

Holding that thought close, she stayed calm as she went with him into the flight office. After he had finished his business there, she walked with him onto the tarmac. The plane should have looked larger close up, but, if anything, the opposite was true. Still, she was composed. She trusted Spencer. He was a veteran pilot. He knew what he was doing. He wouldn't let anything happen to her.

When he stowed her luggage in the back, she widened her eyes on the other things stowed there, a full assortment of bags, boxes and cartons. "What's all that?"

"Supplies. Whenever I'm up here, I buy things to bring back for the house."

Two bags immediately caught her eye. They were a familiar purple color and were filled to the brim. "You were at McCue's?"

"I needed new towels and blankets."

Another bag—not from McCue's—held paper goods. Several others, actually four or five, she guessed, held groceries. She saw a large cooler, a bag filled with books, a combination radio/cassette player still in its box and a bag from Tower Records. "I thought you were in New York on business. From the looks of this, you spent the whole time shopping."

"I did do business."

"Is your manuscript okay now?" She knew that his editor had made him do work even beyond what he had done that weekend at her house.

"Finally." He helped her into the plane, then slid around her into the pilot's seat. As soon as their seat belts were fastened, he began to flip switches. Nonchalantly he said, "You don't look nervous."

"You said I shouldn't be. You said I was safer in this plane than in a commercial jet. You said you were the best pilot around. I'm taking you at your word, Spencer. I'm trusting you with my life." Her voice was nearly as nonchalant as his had been, but her eyes sent him a pointed message.

If he was at all bothered by the responsibility, he didn't show it. "You're a wise woman," he said with confidence, which, under the circumstances, was the best thing he could have done.

Jenna fed off that confidence. It kept her steady during his preflight checks, during the conversation he held with the control tower, during the slow trip out to the runway. At each step, he told her what he was doing. He identified the noises she heard without her having to ask and reassured her that the bumps and vibrations she felt were totally normal.

With surprising ease, the plane was in the air and climbing, and though Jenna's heart was beating faster than normal, she was in no way panicked. Spencer clearly knew what he was doing. He seemed as comfortable at the controls as she was behind the wheel of her car.

"You're doing real well," he said. "I'm proud of you." He reached for her hand and brought it to his mouth for a kiss.

She quickly took it back. "Both hands on the controls, please. You're right, I'm doing real well, but only because you're concentrating fully on this. If you're going to start fooling around, I'll take the first parachute home."

"I don't have parachutes."

"*What?*"

He chuckled. "Just kidding. Not only do I have parachutes, but I packed them myself. I'm an experienced sky diver. Did I ever tell you that?"

"No, but I assumed you've done most everything along that line, like hang gliding, helicopter skiing, hot air ballooning."

His eyes lit up in enthusiasm, confirming the last. "Ever been in a hot air balloon?"

"No."

"You'd love it. It's smooth and silent. Incredibly peaceful."

"It looks a lot simpler than this," she mused with a lost look at the bank of switches and dials.

Spencer shrugged. "This isn't terribly complicated. You could fly it."

"No, thanks. I'll pass."

"I'm serious."

"So am I. You got me up here. Don't push your luck."

He chuckled again, and paid several minutes' attention to the control bank that she found so complex. "I have to say one thing. We got great weather. The flight path all the way down the coast is clear. This time last week Hurricane Chloe was threatening things right and left."

Jenna had followed Chloe's course closely. If the hurricane had gone anywhere near the Keys, she would have been a nervous wreck on Spencer's behalf. "You didn't get much more than rain, did you?"

"Nah."

"But you've lived through far worse."

"Don't you know it. This season is a tough one. If it isn't a hurricane, it's a tropical storm or gale winds or driving rains. That's why salvaging now is out of the question. When the seas get churned up, the dangers multiply, and the seas get churned up this time of year with disgusting regularity." He grunted. "So the judge can take his sweet time coming down with the ruling. We can't do a damn thing in the water until the weather stabilizes." He tapped one of the dials.

Jenna's gaze flew to it. Her pulse faltered. "Any problem?"

"Nope."

"Is that reading okay?"

"It's great."

He sounded confident, which was enough for her. Her pulse leveled. She relaxed as much as she ever relaxed in an airplane, which meant that she was able to take a deep breath, release her death grip on the sides of her seat and quietly put her hands in her lap. The ride wasn't so bad, actually. True, she felt more by way of ups and downs than she would have felt in a larger plane, but Spencer was right, there was a sense of control. Then again, maybe that sense of control came from her faith in him. She doubted there was any other person who could have gotten her on an airplane this size.

"Still with me?" he asked.

"Still with you."

"Not airsick?"

"Not airsick." She waited for him to say I-told-you-so—just as she had waited once before, that first month, when he had told her not to go to Hong Kong. But he hadn't said it then, and he didn't say it now. He was special in that regard, too. Other men made a thing of machismo, of pride and superiority. Spencer didn't, though Lord knew he had better cause to do so. The difference was in self-confidence. Spencer had it. He had earned it. He had proven himself ten times over in the things that mattered to him. She felt such respect for him, *such respect*.

That respect grew even more during the next two hours. Spencer handled the plane as calmly and capably as he handled her. When he made changes at the controls, he told her what he was doing and why, and that included a landing in Savannah that Jenna hadn't realized they would be making. She wasn't pleased when he told her. Takeoffs and landings weren't her cup of tea even in jumbo jets; her travel agent had long since learned to book her a nonstop flight at any cost. But Spencer wasn't her travel agent, and he claimed that even if she didn't have to use the bathroom, the plane needed fuel. She couldn't argue with that.

So they landed in Savannah. He talked her down, then, after they'd availed themselves of the rest rooms, the coffee shop and the fuel tanks, talked her back up into the air. She had to admit that it was easier the second time around, since the sound and feel of the plane were familiar. Still, she knew she wouldn't be completely comfortable until they landed on Spencer's Key. Once she was on the ground there, once she knew that she wouldn't be flying again for two full weeks, she would be able to relax and enjoy Spencer.

Prior to Savannah, they had hugged the coast. Now they flew over water. Jenna put her head back, closed her eyes and, as she always did for the purpose of escape, dozed off. When she awoke, they had just passed to the west of Grand Bahama Island.

It wasn't long after that when she saw a troubled look cross Spencer's face. She wasn't overly alarmed. Surviving four hours in the air, with two takeoffs and a landing, made her something of a veteran. "Something wrong?" she asked casually.

"Nah," he said, and returned his attention to the highway of the sky.

But something about the way he'd said "Nah," as though in annoyance more than conviction, kept her darting him regular looks. Sure enough, several minutes later, he tapped the same dial again and frowned.

"What is it, Spencer? You can tell me. I'm prepared for the worst."

"No worst. This dial has been giving me trouble for the past six months. I've had it replaced twice, but it's still giving cockeyed readings."

"You told me this was a safe plane."

"It is."

"You told me you could sense if anything was wrong even before it showed up on the dials. Do you sense anything wrong?"

"No," he said reasonably. "The plane's flying great. But I also told you I'm a safe pilot, and a safe pilot doesn't ignore a cockeyed reading. We're going in." With the shift of a throttle and the flip of two switches, the plane began to descend.

"In? Where?" Up to then, Jenna had been remarkably calm. Now some of her calmness began to erode. "All I see is water."

"We're coming up on an island." He pointed with a finger that was perfectly steady. "Over there. See it?"

She could make out something vague, barely. "It's a mirage."

"No, it's an island."

"What island is it?" The blob she saw didn't look big enough to allow for a landing, much less repairs on the plane.

"It's just north of Bimini."

"What's it called?"

"Private Island #457."

She stared at him. "Are you serious?"

"Could be #483 or #421. It's hard to tell with these little ones. Did you know that there are seven hundred islands in the Bahamas, and that only thirty of them are inhabited?"

Jenna had a perfectly awful thought. "Are you trying to tell me something, Spencer?"

He grinned. "Yeah, I guess I am. I'm trying to tell you that assuming there's a reasonable stretch of beach, I'm putting down on that little island, and if I do, it's very possible we'll be the only ones there."

"We're putting down on an uninhabited island?" She swallowed hard. "With no runway?"

"A beach is a great runway."

"Spencer," she complained. He didn't seem the least bit upset, which should have been reassuring but wasn't. Her nightmare was coming true.

"Come on, angel," he coaxed gently. "We're in no danger. If this island isn't appropriate to land on, I'll find another. Once we're down, I'll see whether there's any problem. If there is, either I'll fix it myself or radio for help, and if there isn't, we'll take off again with nothing lost but a few minutes."

Jenna was back to gripping the side of her seat, though only with one hand this time. The other hand rested protectively on her stomach. "I should have taken a commercial flight. That was what I wanted to do."

"But you agreed to come with me because you trusted me, and I'm saying that you can trust me still. Do you think dials don't go haywire on commercial jets? Sure they do. But commercial jets can't land on beaches, so they continue on to their destination and a mechanic may take a quick look at the dial between flights. I'm playing it safe."

"By landing on a beach?"

He held up a finger. "Only if the beach looks right. I told you I didn't have a death wish, and I meant it. I also told you that I wouldn't do anything to endanger you, and I meant that, too." He chucked her under the chin.

"This is an adventure, angel. Think of what you'll be able to tell your grandchildren someday."

"Uh-huh," Jenna said with the only energy she had to spare. The rest was being directed toward willing the plane to stay in the air until it reached the island. She imagined she heard all kinds of strange noises coming from the engine. She imagined the air in the cabin felt different. She imagined the plane was losing speed at such an alarming rate that they'd have to put down in the water, which, no doubt, was infested with sharks.

Silently she began to pray. She promised to be good, so good, if only the plane didn't crash. Her life was just beginning. She had so much to live for. She didn't want to die the way her parents had, and she *especially* didn't want to die before she'd had a child. Could fate be that cruel?

"Hanging in there?" Spencer asked.

"Do I have any choice?" she returned in a high-pitched voice.

"Yeah. You could be scrambling around in back hooking on a parachute."

Her eyes widened. "Should I be doing that?"

"Of course not. There's no need for a parachute when we have a perfectly good beach to land on."

She looked out the window. The island had solidified into something resembling a chocolate kiss, but in green. Rimming it was a healthy band of sand. "Are these landings difficult?"

"Nah. Piece a' cake."

She went back to praying. It was either that or yell at Spencer for endangering her life, but that would be counterproductive. He had to concentrate on landing. Then she'd yell.

"Okay," he said with a breath, "now, this landing is going to be exactly the same as the one we made in Savannah." He banked the plane, sending it into an arc that would bring them into alignment with the beach, and he kept talking, just as he'd done during that earlier approach.

Jenna's heart rose to her throat and stayed there this time. Pictures of her life passed before her as the stretch of sand came closer. She thought of her parents, and wondered what they had been thinking in the minutes before their plane had crashed. She thought of her friends and of the people at McCue's, and wondered what would become of the store. She thought about the baby that had such potential—and of *Spencer*, who was so full of life and had so much laughing yet to do. If she hadn't been paralyzed by fright, she might have cried at the loss.

The plane descended the last hundred feet and skimmed the beach for a second before touching down. It bounced once, then a second and third time in quick succession before it finally remained on the ground.

Jenna sat still as stone.

"You can breath now," Spencer said softly. Releasing her seat belt, he drew her rigid body into his arms. "I'm sorry, angel. I know that was tough on you."

"Tough?" she said weakly, then caught a wave of returning strength and said more loudly, "Tough? It was *horrible!*" She struggled out of his arms and glared at him. "How could you *do* this to me, Spencer Smith? You *know* I'm terrified of small planes. You should never have suggested I come on this thing in the *first* place!" Pushing her door open, she scrambled down over the wing and hit the sand at an angry stride.

"Where are you going?" Spencer called, following her out.

"Where *can* I go?" she cried, and kept walking. She had to put space between herself and that plane. She had to gather her wits. So she strode down the beach to an outcrop of large rocks, climbed onto the largest, put her back to Spencer and the plane and sat staring angrily out at sea.

Some time later, Spencer joined her. He didn't touch her, didn't even sit on the rock abutting hers. He chose one that left room between them, which was wise, Jenna realized. Given what he went on to say, had he been closer she would surely have hit him.

"We have a problem," he began.

She pressed her forearms to her thighs.

"The reading on that dial was faulty, all right. There wasn't anything wrong with the hydraulic system. The problem is electrical, which is why that dial was going wild."

She planted her chin on the heels of her hands and gritted her teeth.

"Unfortunately," he went on, "when I turned the engine off just now, the problem that affected the dial caused a larger short circuit that's now affecting far more than one dial. So it looks like we won't be taking right off. That's the good news," he said just as she was thinking it herself. "The bad news is that I don't have the parts I need to fix it. We won't be taking of *at all* until someone gets them to us."

She let out a breath and returned her forearms to her thighs. "How long will it take?"

"That depends," he said in such a hesitant way that her eyes went to his.

"On what?"

"On when we're spotted."

"What do you mean, 'when we're spotted'? Can't you just radio in an alarm?"

He shook his head. "The electrical system is gone."

"Right. That's what you have to tell them."

"I can't tell them. I can't get through. I have no way to contact anyone. The radio is part of the electrical system, and the electrical system is gone. The radio is useless."

Jenna stared at him. "Useless?"

"Nonfunctional. Out of order. Dead."

"I don't believe it," she said.

"Would I kid you about something like that?"

No, she supposed he wouldn't. Slowly the meaning of what he said began to sink in. "Then we're stuck here?"

"'Fraid so."

"For as long as it takes for someone to spot the plane on the beach?"

"Looks that way."

She swallowed. "How long will that be?"

"I don't know. Could be a day or two. Could be longer."

"Longer?"

"A week. Maybe more."

Jenna thought about the last possibility. More than a week could mean a month or two or five. If they were stuck longer than that, she would be significantly pregnant by the time they were found, and all that time, she would be without medical care. She didn't know what she'd do if anything happened to the baby.

"Can we survive here?" she asked nervously.

Spencer didn't look at all nervous, nor did he sound it. "Easily. We've got food. We've got shelter. We've got clothes. We've even got towels and blankets."

"This is the hurricane season. What if it storms?"

"Then we'll sit it out. This island has survived more storms than you and I can count."

"But there's no one alive here. Maybe there's a message in that."

"There's no one alive here because there's nothing to do here."

"What'll *we* do here?"

"We'll eat the food I brought. We'll read the books I bought. We'll lie in the sun. We'll swim." His eyes suddenly sparkled. "I can think of a few other things we can do."

Jenna could, too, and wanted to hit him for reminding her. It was inappropriate to be thinking about sex when their lives were at stake.

She considered telling him she was pregnant. He had a right to know. He had to share the responsibility for the baby's well-being. Then she realized that he didn't have to share the responsibility at all! Papers to that effect, signed by her, were in her lawyer's office. From the first, she had promised she would ask nothing of him but his sperm. She intended to stand by that promise.

So she wouldn't tell him about the baby because it wasn't his responsibility. And because it wouldn't make any difference to their chances for rescue. And because he would be furious that she'd deceived him.

"I should have flown Delta," she muttered.

"Yeah, and you'd have arrived at my place and waited and waited, and I'd still be on this island. So which is better—" he stood "—being alone there waiting or being here with me?" He sauntered off, back in the direction of the plane.

In a fit of fury that was no doubt a legacy of the terror she'd felt during their landing on the beach, she yelled after him, "*There*, Spencer, I'd rather be *there*, and if you're so *arrogant* as to believe it's not true, you're deluding yourself!" She rose with her hands on her hips. "You and your plane have taken ten years off my life. I'll have nightmares about that landing for days, and now I have to worry about surviving to be rescued. Well, let me tell you something, when that rescue plane comes, I don't care if it *does* bring you the parts you need to fix your crate, I'm going back with the rescuers!" She was breathing hard, feeling emotionally strung out. When he kept walking, she yelled louder, "You're not only *arrogant*, you're *sly*. You *conned* me into flying with you. You wanted me to trust you, and I did, and where did it get me?" Even louder. "I'm stuck on a deserted island in the middle of the ocean with a man who spends his life living out his childhood fantasies! *Grow up*, Spencer! Life isn't all Spanish galleons, sparkling gold and sex!"

By the time she ran out of strength and breath, he had stopped walking. He stood with his head bowed for a minute before slowly turning. Just as slowly but with purpose, he started back toward her, and the closer he came, the more uneasy she grew. He looked furious. She was grateful that she stood on her rock, which gave her a small height advantage. Then she wondered whether even that would help. With his black hair strewn over his forehead, his brows drawn together and his jaw set in such a way that his scar seemed to pulse, he looked like an angry man, indeed.

Had her pride allowed it, she would have stepped back. But she was Jenna McCue, president and chairman of the board of McCue's. She was a woman of reason and, perhaps, momentary temper, but she was also the mother-to-be of Spencer Smith's child—even if he didn't know it yet—and she refused to cower. She tipped up her chin and met his gaze as bravely as she could.

Halting at the base of her rock, he stared at her for a minute. Then, before she realized what he planned and could ward him off, he ducked his shoulder and swung her over it. Stunned, she had to fight to catch her breath, but by the time she could launch a protest, he was striding boldly back to the plane.

10

"PUT ME DOWN!" she cried. "Spencer, you can't *do* this! Put me down!"

He kept walking.

The blood was rushing to her head, making it feel thick and heavy. "I mean it, Spencer!" She clutched fistfuls of his shirt to keep from bouncing with his stride. "Put me down!"

His arm was an unyielding band behind her knees. It held her firmly and, at the same time, prevented her from kicking. Not that she'd have done that. She was suddenly very upset—upset that the plane wouldn't fly, upset that they couldn't call for help, upset that Spencer was angry, upset that she'd said such awful things. She was upset about the baby, too, because the last thing she wanted was to expose it to risk, but she had. It was her fault, all her fault. If she hadn't lied to Spencer, he wouldn't have invited her south, and if he hadn't invited her south, they wouldn't be stranded on a uninhabited island with no rescue in sight.

Feeling dizzy and overwhelmed, she started to cry. She pressed her cheek to his back. "Please—Spencer—I'm sorry."

The words were barely out of her mouth, when he bent forward and let her slip from his shoulder. When he saw her tears, he swore. He lifted her in his arms this time, and, while she pressed her face to his throat, carried her to the inland edge of the beach where the sea grass began. Palm trees grew there, curving upward. An umbrella of fronds spread at their tops, while their bottoms swirled around and broadened into inviting benches. Spencer straddled one, seating Jenna between his legs. He kept an arm curved around her, holding her close.

"Don't cry on me, angel," he said in a gruff voice. "I can't take it when you cry. I swear, I'd rather listen to the chant of a band of headhunters than to hear that sobbing. Shh. Come on, Jenna. Shh. You've gone teary eyed on me twice before, once when you thought I wouldn't donate my sperm, then again when I told you I would, and both times the sight of those tears got to me. Now it's the whole shebang. But hell, I'm the one who should be upset. I'm the one who was called all kinds of names."

"I know." She brushed the tears away. "I'm sorry. I shouldn't have called you those names. I was wrong." Her eyes filled again. She pressed her face more tightly to his shirt so that he wouldn't have to see.

Still gruffly, he said, "There's no need to be upset. We aren't in any danger."

"We're marooned."

"We're probably less than one hundred miles from Miami."

"But we can't get there."

"So? We're safe, and we have supplies."

"But for how long? Oh, Spencer, if it hadn't been for me, you wouldn't be here."

"How do you figure that? I was in New York, anyway. I had to fly home."

"But you'd have ignored that dial, and you'd have gotten home just fine. The electrical system didn't blow out until you landed. The plane was flying well until then. You only took it down to prove to me what a cautious pilot you were." When he didn't say anything, she said, "Isn't that so?"

"Yeah, but it's water over the dam. I'm not upset we're here, Jenna."

"But we could be here *forever*." She had visions of giving birth to the baby on the beach without knowing what to do. She was a businesswoman by training, not a midwife. All the reading she'd done had dealt with getting pregnant, not giving birth. She hadn't been to the doctor since she'd missed her period. She certainly hadn't started childbirth classes yet.

"We won't be here forever," Spencer scolded.

"How do you know?"

"Because I know these islands. Planes fly over them all the time. Cruise boats sail past them. Charters work through these waters and put in at islands like this one for cookouts on the beach."

"During hurricane season?" she asked skeptically.

"During every season if the money is right. Okay, if there's a hurricane brewing, they don't go. But there's no hurricane brewing this week, so someone will find us."

"Before we run out of food?"

"We won't ever run out of food. Between bananas and fish, we have an endless supply."

"Bananas?"

"In the forest. And I have brand-new fishing gear in the plane."

Jenna figured a baby might like bananas, but there was *no way* it would like fish. She had hated it for the first twenty-three years of her life. Of course, she planned to breast-feed the baby for a good long time, and since she liked both bananas and fish just fine now, perhaps the issue of starvation was moot. Other issues were not.

"What about everyone back home?" she asked. "They'll assume we crashed. Can you imagine what that will do to Caroline, and your parents? And the company? They'll hold memorial services." She moaned. "It would be *awful*."

He gave her a squeeze. "Don't rush things, angel. Your people aren't expecting you back for two weeks, so they won't start worrying until then, and my people know not to miss me for a lot longer than that. I've disappeared before and shown up alive too many times for anyone to think twice, and that *especially* means my family. Caroline knows you're with me." Jenna had told her they were spending some time together. "She'll assume I did exactly what I did—that I set down on an uninhabited island so that I could have you to myself for two weeks."

Jenna wiped her eyes on his shirt. "I wish you wouldn't say things like that."

"Why not?"

"Because they're sweet. But you're not supposed to be sweet. You're supposed to be a brash swashbuckler."

His arms relaxed. "Sorry to disappoint you, angel. Hey, why don't you come exploring with me? I want to see what we're working with. Are you game?"

She raised her eyes. If Spencer was at all worried about getting back to civilization, there was no evidence of it on his face. He looked as though he'd merely stopped by the island for an afternoon's adventure. But, then, adventuring was his thing. He was good at it. He loved doing it.

To please him, she said, "Okay."

He wiped the last traces of tears from her face and grinned. "That's my girl." Helping her to her feet, he led her off down the beach.

They passed the plane with its engine open where he had been working. They passed a dozen palms like the one they had been sitting on. Spencer stopped occasionally to peer toward the thicker growth, but it wasn't until they'd reached the end of the beach that he led her in.

Jenna wanted the woods to be breathtakingly beautiful, which was the way woods should be, she reasoned, if one had to be marooned near them. But these woods weren't beautiful. She wasn't even sure she could call them woods. The shrubbery was about Spencer's height and nondescript. Other than the palm trees, she might have been back in Rhode Island.

As they advanced inland, however, things began to grow. The path started to steepen. The trees greened and spread skyward. Though Spencer held her hand, Jenna kept watch underfoot for vines that were easily tripped on. She also kept watch for snakes and other crawling things that, once seen, would surely keep her from sleeping. When Spencer saw the vigilant way she was walking and asked, she bluntly told him her fear. He assured her that there would be no snakes, and that if there were lizards about, they were harmless. As though to make his point, he indicated the disappearing tail of one such creature, which, he claimed, was more afraid of them then they could ever be of it. Jenna wasn't so sure, but she nodded.

They walked on. Their sneakers made little noise on the forest floor, compared to the buzz of insects and the occasional cry of a bird. Spencer pointed out various forms of vegetation, but he seemed to be listening.

When they came to a clearing, he broke into a grin. Victoriously he said, "I thought I smelled water." Sure enough, the clearing was bisected by a tiny stream.

"Smelled?"

"It's distinct." He knelt beside the stream, cupped a handful of water and sipped it. With his eyes, he invited Jenna to join him.

She was thirsty and very warm. Kneeling, she drank her fill of the clear, fresh water, then patted it to her face, neck, throat and wrists. It felt heavenly.

Spencer watched her. "It's hot in here. The air doesn't move as much as it does on the beach. Want to head back?"

"Not if you want to explore more." She refused to slow him down, and, in truth, it felt good to walk. She would walk, rather than fly, any day. On this particular day, walking worked the tension of the flight and its premature landing from her body.

But Spencer seemed bent on turning back. "I'll explore more another time. I'm hungry."

"You're always hungry," she said, but looking at his long, lean shape through his clothes, remembering the feel of his bare body in the dark, she doubted he carried an ounce of fat.

"Aren't you?" he asked.

"Not always."

"Are you now?"

"A little." Actually, she was more than a little. She was famished. She wondered if it had anything to do with the baby and prayed that it didn't. Their supply of food was limited. Despite Spencer's claim of unlimited bananas and fish, she was going to have to watch what she ate. If she ate wisely and as balanced a diet as possible, the baby would be fine.

The return trip to the beach seemed shorter. The fact that it was downhill helped, as did the breeze, which gusted toward them more often as they neared the water, lessening the effect of the heat.

Spencer declared himself chef. Claiming that certain of the foods he'd brought would only keep a short time without refrigeration, he made two overstuffed ham-and-cheese sandwiches—on croissants from a Manhattan bakery, no less, Jenna mused. For dessert, he produced a chocolate cake from the cooler, which also held six-packs of beer and Evian water.

"Boy," Jenna said, studying the cooler and its contents, "when you get marooned, you do it in style." And in style, they did it. They ate on a large beach towel beneath the shade of a cluster of palm trees whose fronds rippled in the breeze. The sound was as peaceful as the gently rhythmic one of the sea rolling onto the shore. Closing her eyes and listening, Jenna could almost forget that she was stranded on an uninhabited island for the indefinite future.

Almost. But not quite. Each time she thought of it, she felt renewed unease. It would be one thing if she knew she was here for, say, three days or even a week. She could handle that. But indefinitely? That was a frightening thought.

Spencer apparently didn't share her fear. As soon as he had had his fill of lunch, he stretched out on his back with his shoulder touching her thigh, laced his hands on his middle, crossed his ankles and went to sleep. He looked perfectly calm, totally relaxed and eminently content.

While he slept, Jenna studied him, as she had never had quite the occasion to do before. She admired his feet, which were bare now. Her gaze climbed his long, hair-roughened legs to his shorts, which lay on his lean hips in such a way that his sex was pronounced. Her eyes lingered there for a long time, before she dragged them over his T-shirt, which broadened with his chest, to his neck, then his face. The beginnings of a dark shadow had appeared on his jaw. She wondered whether he would shave while they were there. She wondered whether he would bathe in the ocean. She wondered whether he would have her cut his hair when it grew shaggy and long.

But damn it, she wasn't a barber any more than she was a midwife. She had never been a Girl Scout. She had never gone camping. When it came to outdoor things, she had enthusiasm but little experience. In that respect, the thought of what lay ahead in the next few days, perhaps weeks or months, was thoroughly daunting.

It galled her that Spencer didn't feel any of that. He had simply eaten his lunch and gone to sleep as though he had nothing better to do. But he did! He could be working on the plane. He claimed he didn't have the parts to repair it, but maybe with enough tinkering, something would start. He could *try*, at least.

And if he didn't want to work on the engine, he could be taking inventory of their supplies for the purpose of rationing. It was one thing to have huge sandwiches and chocolate cake on the first day they were marooned, if for no other reason than to boost their spirits. But if they continued to eat so freely, they might be very sorry two or three weeks down the road.

And if he didn't want to be taking inventory, he could be building a shelter. The plane might be fine for protection during a brief rainstorm, but they couldn't very well sleep there. They wouldn't be able to stretch out.

For a prolonged period, they needed more room. She would go at it herself if she had any idea what to do, but she didn't. Roughing it was Spencer's specialty, not hers. But Spencer was sleeping as soundly as a child, and for the life of her she couldn't wake him.

So she brooded. She glared at his serene features and wondered how a man could so lackadaisically accept his fate. She shifted her gaze to the sea and scanned the horizon. Cruise ships passed by, he had said. Charters came for cookouts. But she didn't see anything that remotely resembled a boat, and as for airplanes passing overhead, the sky was clear blue and empty. It occurred to her that since they had landed nearly three hours before, she hadn't heard even a single drone of another airplane.

So much for airplanes flying overhead all the time!

And Spencer slept on.

Needing to do something, Jenna bounded up and started down the beach. She walked along the lip of the sand, just shy of the beach grass, where pieces of driftwood had gathered. She collected them until her arms were filled, then carried them back and formed a pile on the highest spot of sand near the airplane, where the tide wouldn't go. If a boat or a plane passed by at dawn, at dusk or during the night, they'd need a bonfire. Even a noncamper knew that. Spencer had matches. Now they had wood.

Sending intermittent scowls Spencer's way, she took strength from self-righteous efficiency. Back and forth she went until she had a sizable pile of wood, at which point the unfortunate realization hit that if it rained, the wood would get wet and be useless. So she transferred it, armload by armload, into a haphazard pile under the plane. By this time her shorts and shirt were dirty, she had chipped the polish off the tips of two fingernails, her hair was fast falling from its pins and she was sweaty. But at least *someone* had done something practical, she mused, then whirled around when Spencer's booming voice broke the island's peace.

"What are you *doing?*" He was bounding to his feet with a furious look on his face. "Just because the electrical system's bad doesn't mean the whole thing's no good. What in the hell will you accomplish by *burning* it?"

"I'm not burning it," Jenna snapped, "though I should for all the good it's done us. I was gathering wood, and that seemed like the only place to store it where it won't get wet if it rains. If anything passes nearby, we'll need a signal fire."

His anger faded instantly. He ran a hand over his face, as though belatedly waking up, then pushed that hand through his hair. "Good thinking." He eyed her more closely and with a touch of a smile. "That really was good thinking. I'm proud of you, Jenna."

She didn't like his smile. It suggested surprise that she had a head on her shoulders, and was as chauvinistic as anything she'd seen him do. "Well, someone has to think around here." She tossed a hand toward the towel. "You eat until you're stuffed, then fall into a sleep so deep that it would take an army to wake you, and in the meantime, our rescuers would have come and gone."

He let out a breath. "Uh-oh, you're worked up again?"

"Someone has to be, or we'll never get out of here."

"What's your rush?"

She pointed in the direction she thought home might be, though in fact she couldn't have said where north was. "I have a life back there. I have things to do. I can't spend the next few years of my life eating fish and bananas on a tropical island."

He let out a bored sigh. "It's not tropical. We're not even in the Caribbean. This is the Atlantic."

She arched a brow. "Are people rescued from the Atlantic more often than from the Caribbean?"

"Come on, Jenna."

"I want to be rescued," she stated. "I'm not the hardened adventurer you are. I'm not used to being in precarious situations like you are. You love the mystery of it, the challenge, but not me. I like security. I like stability. I *like* knowing where I'll be a month from now." She gave a short headshake. "I can't take things like this in stride the way you can. I can't just turn over and go to sleep and wait for fate to happen. I have to *do* something."

He ducked his head until he was on eye level with her and said in an exasperated way, "But there isn't anything *to* do."

"We can build a fire."

"Not in broad daylight. Besides, I have a flare gun in the plane. A single shot'll do it if anything passes nearby."

She was still for a minute. "You have a flare gun. I've spent half my afternoon gathering wood for a fire, and you have a flare gun. That's just great!" Whirling around, she stalked past the towel. "You could have told me." She plopped down on the base of the palm.

He followed her. "You didn't ask."

"How could I ask? You went to sleep."

"Well, I was tired. You think you're the only one who feels tension? Maybe, just maybe that landing was hard on me, too."

Jenna wasn't in the mood to feel sorry for him. "I don't buy that. You thrive on danger. For the ten years I lost during that landing, you probably gained five."

"If I did, you're taking them away real quick. For God's sake, Jenna, ease up," he muttered, and started unbuttoning his shirt. "This isn't the end of the world."

Her eyes fell to his chest, which was fast appearing. "What are you doing?"

"Going swimming. In case you haven't noticed, it's hot here."

"And you've been working so hard."

"I don't work hard unless there's good reason to work hard, and there isn't. Not here. Not now." He pulled his arms from the sleeves and tossed the shirt aside. "We have supplies and shelter, and all the time in the world." He undid his shorts. "If you want to scurry around seeing to all kinds of little domestic chores, be my guest." He pushed down the shorts and his briefs and stepped out of them. "Just don't ask me to help." Stark naked and totally unselfconscious, he cocked his hands on his hips. "I'll be the first one to fix a meal or set up a tarp or dig a latrine, but I refuse to go looking for other work. I don't need routine. I don't need chores to keep me happy. If I'm stuck here, I intend to make the most of it. I intend to have fun."

Jenna swallowed and shifted in her seat. She was trying desperately to keep her eyes above his neck, but she was abundantly aware of what lay below. She had touched it. She knew the texture of the hair there, and the firmness of his flesh when he was aroused.

"Go ahead," he goaded. "Look. I'm not shy."

"That's obvious," she said, but she kept her eyes on his. What she saw there was nearly as unsettling as what she was seeing below his waist. Those blue eyes gleamed. They were suddenly filled with a brand of mischief that had danger etched in silver, and they were coming closer. With smooth, deliberate movements, he approached, leaned over and propped his hands on either side of her hips.

His breath was gentle against her cheek. "I dare you, Jenna. I dare you to look at me." He remained bent that way, letting his lips play by her ear.

Unable to resist, she looked down at his body. Her chest tightened at the sight of him. He was large and bold, suspended so beautifully that he might have been sculpted by a master—which indeed he had been, she mused. By way of resisting the urge to touch him, she pressed her hands to the palm trunk.

Slowly he straightened and took a step back. She kept looking at him, curious and fascinated, impressed, aroused.

"I dare you, Jenna" came his low voice. "Dare you to take off your clothes and swim with me." Her eyes flew to his face, and everything she saw there reinforced the dare. "Dare you to let me see you naked."

Her heart was beating soft and fast, a tiny animal caught between danger and desire. She swallowed again. Her eyes were wide on his.

Then he gave her the indolent blink of a tomcat, turned and set off toward the water, calling calmly over his shoulder, "You know where to find me."

She sat there trembling, watching him go. She had seen him naked from behind before, but not with the sun glancing off his bronzed skin and not with the sparkle of the water setting his tall, tapering shape into stark relief. The sheer magnificence of him took her breath away.

In an attempt to restore it, she leaned forward and hugged her knees. From that position, she watched him enter the water. He waded until the waves reached his thighs, then dove shallowly and began a strong over-arm stroke away from shore.

He was right, she knew. She hated to admit it, because her own success in life had come from analyzing a situation and taking action, but in this situation there wasn't much action to take. If Spencer felt that tinkering with the engine would get them anywhere, he would do it. She did believe that he knew his plane forward and backward. If he said they were grounded until he got parts, it was true.

So what were they to do in the meantime? Not much. They could sit and fret over their situation, or make the most of it. Dragging her eyes from his dark head and the arms that stroked steadily through the water, she took stock of the setting. In its own way, the island was beautiful. Though it wasn't as lush as some of the islands she'd visited, it had a natural appeal. It was quiet and peaceful. Its sand was soft and white, its water a translucent turquoise. The air was clean, the breeze refreshing. If she had ever wanted a private setting in which to be with Spencer, she couldn't have asked for one more so.

The danger was there, the same danger that had been present since the day Spencer had announced he would father her child. Jenna had always been slightly in awe of him. From the first night they had come together, she had feared that the awe might grow into something deeper. And it had—so much so, that she who never lied had lied about not being pregnant so that she could have more time with him.

Should the lie go to waste? Should she fritter away her time with him worrying about getting back to civilization? Or should she give him her ultimate trust, take his word that they'd get back and have a good time with him here?

She could end up loving him more. That was the danger now. If it happened, her suffering would be even worse than it would already be when their time here was done and they went their own ways. Then again, if it happened, she would have memories to cherish, memories to someday pass on to her child about the atmosphere in which it had been made.

She looked back at the water. Spencer was swimming parallel to the shore now, doing a strong breast stroke. As she watched, he turned onto his back. One muscled arm followed the other in confident overarm rhythm. He was clearly relaxed and enjoying himself. She wanted to be relaxed, too. She wanted to enjoy herself. If the most she could have was memories, damn it, she wanted them.

Pushing herself to her feet, she began to undress. She put her clothes in a neat pile, thinking about habits that were hard to break, like neatness and modesty. Spencer was doing the front crawl again, so he couldn't see her, still the touch of the breeze on her bare skin made her acutely aware of her nakedness, as did the kiss of the sun on virgin curves as she set out for the water. She went faster than Spencer had, seeking the shelter of the waves. The water was bathtub warm. She dove under and came up with her head back. Her hair streamed away from her forehead and down her shoulders, those few pins that had remained in it lost to the surf. She stroked away from shore, then treaded water until she caught sight of Spencer. He was swimming toward her, his head above water, his arms beneath. The surf helped him along. He kept his eyes on her.

She continued to tread water. When he was an arm's length away, he let his feet sink until he, too, was upright in the water. As they bobbed gently before each other, his eyes asked a silent question, then lowered to the water's surface in search of the answer. Jenna had only to look through the waves herself at the hair clearly visible midway down his chest to know what he was seeing.

Guiding himself with purposeful scissor kicks, he came closer and ran his hands from her shoulders, down her back and over her buttocks. With the revelation that she wasn't wearing even bikini bottoms, his blue eyes seemed to take on the life of the sea. She kept hers fastened to them, taking encouragement as it was needed.

"Hold on to my shoulders," he urged. At the same time, he gave her hips a gentle push toward the surface. When she was prone, he began a breast stroke that propelled her backward. Not once did his eyes leave hers.

She knew the instant he was able to stand. He touched a foot to the ocean floor, then kicked off again and swam on a little longer so that when he stood this time, the water came to midchest. Just as her own legs started to sink, he brought her against him.

She wrapped her arms tightly around his neck and closed her eyes. This was what she wanted—the closeness, the feel of his body against her, the strength of his arms around her. She felt secure and savored. She felt wanted for who she was as she had come to him, totally unadorned.

He continued to walk until the water lapped at his waist. Reaching back, he took her arms from around his neck and eased her down to her feet. His gaze fell to her breasts, which floated just above the waterline. His face darkened with desire.

He didn't say a word. He didn't have to. His eyes touched her with a reverence that gave her the courage to let him look his fill, and where courage left off, pleasure picked up. That surprised her. She hadn't anticipated feeling pleasure when he looked at her. She hadn't expected to feel proud or aroused, yet she felt both.

Drawing his hands from the water, he touched her breasts with his fingertips. He traced her roundness, then cupped her fullness with his palm and gave his thumbs free rein. They slid over her wet flesh first on the outer swell of her, then progressively inward until, just when Jenna was about to go wild with frustration, they covered her nipples.

She didn't even try to contain the sound of aching pleasure that came from her throat. Spencer looked at her as though she was a woman. He touched her as though she was a woman. The fact that she cried out like one was normal and acceptable, even desirable, if the expression of satisfaction on his face meant anything. Moving his hands to her hips, he walked her backward until the water fell away from first her ribs, then her waist, then her navel. He paused to watch the sea skim her. He spread his fingers, moved his palms. He walked her backward another few steps until her thighs emerged, and stood for the longest time with his gaze locked on the dark triangle at their apex. Then, taking a slow route that caressed her at each stop, his eyes rose to hers.

"Don't ever hide from me again, Jenna," he murmured. "You're too beautiful to play that game."

She couldn't speak, couldn't take her eyes from his face. The look there was everything she could have ever wanted, and though she didn't fool herself into thinking that it would last longer than their stay on the island, she basked in it now. It gave her the confidence to rise on her toes and initiate the kind of long, soul kiss that she hadn't liked from other men, much less been able to give.

He rewarded her by sinking to his knees in the surf and bringing her down over his lap. She felt him rise inside her to fill the aching void that had been, and there, with the ocean playing gently around their legs, he loved her as she had never dreamed to be loved. She touched him and offered herself to be touched. She opened her mouth wide to his, opened her body wide to his. She couldn't seem to get or give enough, and when they both climaxed, when their sharp gasps had mellowed into softer pants of satisfaction, she knew that she'd made the right decision.

For as long as they were on the island, she was Spencer's. He was the fantasy she had never dared entertain, and even if there would be pain at the end, she was going for the pleasure now. She owed it to Spencer as a thank-you for giving her a child. She owed it to the child as a source of memories of its father to warm long winter nights. Mostly, though, she owed it to herself. She was a woman. Mothering a child would be one source of fulfillment. Being with Spencer was another.

11

PARADISE WAS an uninhabited island, after all, Jenna decided several nights later as she lay in Spencer's arms. He had made a bed by scattering fern fronds on the sand, covering them with towels and rolling blankets into pillows. He had even stretched a tarp from the body of the plane to its wing to provide shelter should it rain during the night.

It had rained that afternoon, a quick island rain that came for an hour and left when the dark cloud passed by. Rather than taking shelter, they had walked the beach. When their clothes had been drenched, they'd taken them off and continued on naked. Jenna had never done anything like that before and was still stunned by the sense of ultimate freedom in it. She doubted she'd forget that, or the caress of the rain on her bare skin, for as long as she lived.

At the moment, though, rain seemed unlikely. A half-moon was shimmering over the water, silvering the linings of the occasional clouds that passed by. The sea lapped the shore with fair-weather ease. It was a calm, quiet night.

They had cooked dinner—steak from the cooler and potatoes—over a fire made with Jenna's wood. The flame had long since died, leaving an orange glow on the sand not far from where they lay. She was on her side against him, with her cheek on his chest and a leg between his, while he held her close with a single firm arm. Though she wore one of his shirts and he wore shorts, the memory of flesh against flesh, as it had been so often in the three days since they'd landed on the beach, kept them warm.

It occurred to Jenna that she had never felt so peaceful or content in her life, which was particularly remarkable since there had been no sign of a cruise ship, a sailboat or a rescue plane. She should have been worried. But she wasn't. It was too early to worry. She was having too fine a time with Spencer.

"What are you thinking?" he asked against her hair.

"How far away Rhode Island feels. Not just physically. Emotionally. Like it's another world. Like I've been through a time warp."

"That was the trauma of the landing."

"The landing wasn't so bad," she said because he sounded disturbed. Yes, she'd been upset. In hindsight, though, there hadn't been a point when she had truly believed they would crash. Spencer had been in control of the plane the entire time. "I think it's more the difference between here and there. Here, there's no sense of time. Life is slow and leisurely. We do what we want, when we want. There, life goes according to schedule."

"Tell me more about that life, Jenna. About what a day is like."

She moved her cheek against his chest, loving the feel of the hair there, loving the firmness of his flesh, loving the way he asked questions. As an adventurer, he was naturally curious, but she'd never thought his curiosity would extend to the details of her life. Yet this wasn't the first time he'd asked.

"My day is very organized," she began. "My secretary types up a schedule before she leaves the office each day, so that when I arrive the next morning, I know just what to do. Sometimes I have reports to read. Mostly I'm busy with meetings and phone calls."

"Where are the meetings?"

"Sometimes in my office. Sometimes in our conference room. Sometimes in restaurants. *Often* in restaurants," she amended dryly. "Businessmen love an excuse to eat in style and deduct the meal."

"Business*men*. What about business*women*?"

"Not us. We're always on diets. We'd be just as happy to meet in our offices. That's the safest place."

"Because of the food?"

"Because of the men. In an office, clear lines are drawn. I sit at my desk—whoever I'm meeting sits on the other side. In a restaurant, those lines become blurred. I feel more threatened with men in restaurants."

"That's because you're single."

"I assume."

"Which still amazes me. I can't believe some terrific guy hasn't come along and swept you off your feet."

She sputtered out a soft laugh. "The terrific guys aren't sitting around the city wangling meals on expense accounts. They're in the Himalayas looking for Noah's ark, or retracing Peary's expedition over the Pole, or exploring the Amazon." She gave him a teasing pinch.

He didn't laugh. Soberly he asked, "What makes those guys terrific?"

"They're activists. They're nonconformists. They're interesting." She sighed, knowing what she had to say next. "And they're off-limits, which makes them all the more attractive. But going after them is like trying to catch the wind. Stopping them would be like caging a wild bird." Which was just how she felt. She was head over heels in love with Spencer, but she would never ground him, much less try. She knew how he resented his parents. She refused to make the mistakes they'd made. Spencer's adventures were too important to him to even *hint* that he give them up.

Besides, just because she was madly in love with him, that didn't mean he felt anything beyond attraction and affection for her.

She forced out a sigh. "Anyway, I told you at the start that I wasn't looking for a husband. I don't need one. I have my life under control."

He was quiet for a minute. "I wonder how we're doing with the baby stuff. We've thrown your rules out the window."

"I know." They had been making love whenever and in whatever position they wanted, with no thought at all to what was best for conception. But, then, Jenna knew it didn't matter. Likewise, she hadn't brought her thermometer along. When Spencer had asked her about it, she had said—sheepishly—that she'd known they would be making love often during their time together, so knowing the exact day she was ovulating didn't matter. In truth, she hadn't wanted Spencer to see that her temperature hadn't dipped at all that month. As close as she could guess, she was four weeks pregnant.

"You're not worried it won't happen, are you?" he asked.

"It'll happen."

He was quiet again for a time before asking, with a kind of reluctant curiosity, "Do you think about the baby much? I mean, not about getting pregnant, but about the baby itself?"

She was surprised and pleased that he'd asked. "I think about it a lot."

"Do you want a boy or a girl?"

She tipped her head back to meet his eyes. "I'm supposed to say that it doesn't matter as long as the baby is healthy, and the largest part of me truly feels that way."

"The other part?"

"Wants a girl."

"Why?"

She returned her cheek to his chest. Lightly, so that he wouldn't think she was complaining, criticizing or, worse, making a subtle suggestion, she said, "For one thing, I imagine it would be harder raising a boy without a father figure around. Not impossible. Just harder. For another, there's the issue of companionship. There's mutual identity with a child of the same sex."

"There's also competition. Caroline and my mother used to go at it for hours. Didn't you and your mother argue?"

"Sometimes. It wasn't so bad. I guess because I was an only child, she indulged me. And because they were gone a lot."

"Where did they go?"

"Here and there. They traveled for the business, and whenever they could they tacked on a few extra days. Second honeymoons, they called them." She smiled. "I think they must have had a hundred second honeymoons over the years. They were very much in love. They were each other's best friends." Her smile faded into pensiveness. "I suppose if they had to die early, they were better off dying together. If one had been left without the other, the pain would have been unbearable."

"It's rare to find two people who love like that."

"Mmm."

"Did you ever wish for something similar?"

"All I want is a baby."

"Right now. But other times. Have you ever dreamed of finding that kind of love?"

His natural curiosity notwithstanding, Jenna was still surprised to find Spencer talking about love. Most men didn't. Most men were uncomfortable discussing it. They used the term, usually in bed before or after sex, but when a woman asked what they meant, they closed up like clams. Spencer, on the other hand, was pursuing the discussion. She felt she owed him an honest answer.

"I've dreamed of finding love," she said quietly. "I used to dream of it all the time. Then it didn't come, so I told myself I could do without."

"Can you?"

"I'll have to, won't I?" she said with a laugh that was supposed to be nonchalant but fell short.

Spencer didn't answer. When he finally spoke, he asked another question. "Will the rest of your life be enough to compensate?"

"If I have a baby, it will."

He was skeptical. "Even with a baby?"

"Yes."

"And when the baby grows up and moves out?"

They had touched on that issue in one of their earliest talks, back in Rhode Island, when Jenna was trying to explain why she wanted a baby so badly. Since then she had fallen in love with Spencer. He would be leaving her, too, which made the question and its answer even more apt. "When the baby—child—adult moves out, I'll still have the business, but it's not like

I'll cease being a parent. There's a saying to the effect that a parent is a parent for the rest of her life. I'll certainly always love this child. I'll always feel a responsibility for it. With a little luck, he or she and I will always be close."

"Would you want another one?"

She caught her breath. "Ahh. A pregnant question if ever there was one."

"Would you? If you had that love of your life so that finding a sperm donor wasn't an issue, would you have more than one child?"

Without hesitancy, she said, "Yes. I'd have at least two or three. If I had that love of my life, I'd want to go off with him, too, but I wouldn't want a child of mine to feel the loneliness I felt. Not that I'm criticizing my parents. They always left me well attended. But I missed them when they were gone. If I'd had a brother or sister, it mightn't have been so bad." She sighed. "But that really is beside the point. I'll be content with one child. We'll keep each other company."

SEVERAL DAYS LATER, Spencer surprised her by raising the issue of the baby again. They were sitting in the wet sand at the water's edge, playing with small shells and seaweed, not so much drawing pictures as doodling. The fun came when every few minutes a strong wave washed over their markings, leaving behind something far more interesting and attractive than what they'd started with. Of course, it was changed again with the next wave, and diminished with each successive one, but that didn't matter. They simply started all over again.

"When you think about the baby," he asked, "do you think about doing things like this?"

She hadn't been thinking about the baby then. She hadn't even been thinking about Spencer, though he was her partner in art. She had been engrossed in the activity, feeling lighthearted and carefree. Would she do things like this with the baby? "I'd love to. Children are fascinated with the way the sand changes." She laughed when a new wave rolled in. "*I'm* fascinated with it. Look." She bent a knee to let the surf roll past and watched the new design emerging in the sand.

"You live on the shore. You see this all the time."

"But you know our sand. It's different. Harder. Besides, I don't think I've ever sat like this at home. I've never taken the time. Once the baby comes, I will." Assuming she made it back to Rhode Island. The fact that not even the smallest sailboat had passed by made her uneasy from time to time. But Spencer said they would be rescued, so they would be rescued. If he wasn't worried, she wouldn't be, either. It was far more fun to set new shells in her sand design.

Oddly enough, he seemed worried about the baby. "Won't it make you nervous raising a small child so close to the water?"

"You were raised close to the water. So was I. Neither of us drowned."

"I came damned close more than once. My parents never let me forget it. They claim they should have known what kind of person I'd grow up to be when I kept tempting fate that way. What if you have a little boy like me?"

She grinned at him. "I'd love to have a little boy like you."

"He'll give you gray hair."

"Maybe not. Maybe he'll keep me young."

"You are young. Very young."

"Only six years younger than you."

"Right now, you look about twelve years old." His gaze touched her breasts. "Make that fourteen." He frowned and pushed himself to his feet. "You're turning red. I'll get the sun block." He headed back toward the plane.

Jenna watched him for a minute. She was glad his swim trunks weren't the miniscule swatches of fabric he'd worn on Crete years before. Skimpy bikinis were fine on teenagers and men in their twenties, but Spencer's stature called for something more classy. The bathing suit he wore was that. It was like a pair of snug-fitting boxers and did his body proud.

Boy, was he right about her, though. The preparations she had made for the trip—manicure and pedicure, facial, haircut—might never have been. Had it not been for her breasts, she would have looked much younger indeed, and she didn't need a mirror to tell her. She wore no makeup, no jewelry. On her head, to shade her eyes from the sun, was Spencer's baseball cap, with her ponytail spilling through the hole in the back. Her bikini—of which she wore only the bottom—was from the junior department, and why not? She was making up for lost time. When she'd been a teenager, she'd been too plump to wear anything brief. For a long time after she'd slimmed down, she had continued to *feel* fat, imagining folds in her skin where her friends assured her there were none. Gradually she had grown comfortable in higher-cut one-piece suits. Only in the past few years had she worn bikinis, and then only in select company.

Spencer was as select as company got. He had seen her in nothing at all more times now than she could count. He didn't leer. He simply enjoyed looking at her.

She had the impression that what he enjoyed nearly as much as seeing her body was her having the confidence to show it unclothed.

She'd come a long way, she thought with a smile, and watched him return to her over the sand. He squatted so that she was between his knees, dabbed sun block across her shoulder blades, recapped the tube, then began to rub the cream into her skin.

"You take good care of me," she said, feeling pampered.

"Sun poisoning isn't any fun."

"I thought I was turning brown."

"You are. Under the red."

His able hands kneaded, spreading the sun block over her shoulders, back and chest. He lingered long enough on her breasts to stir her deeper. In an achy voice, she said, "Are you trying to tell me something, Spencer?" His slightest touch made her ready for love, and it didn't matter whether it was midnight or high noon. She had grown positively shameless.

He rubbed his forearm under her breasts, lifting them slightly. "These always surprise me. I knew from touching them that they were firm, but I hadn't pictured them as being as big as they are."

They were bigger than they'd been the month before, and Jenna knew why. Her stomach was as flat as ever, though, which meant that Spencer wouldn't guess her condition. When she didn't get her period in ten days, he would know, but that was fine. It would be the best way for him to find out. After all, he wouldn't know if the baby came a month early. He wouldn't be around then.

"When you touch me," she said softly, "I swell. When you're anywhere *near* me, I swell."

He pressed his mouth to her nape. His palms moved in large, stroking circles, one on her back, one on her stomach. After a minute, he drew in a shuddering breath. "Oh, God."

Something in his tone frightened her, and it went beyond the pain of arousal. She looked up. "What's wrong?"

His silver-blue eyes flashed. "I want you. I always want you. I should be getting past this, but I'm not."

As admissions went, it was heart stopping because there was bewilderment in it, and bewilderment wasn't something Jenna normally associated with Spencer. He was always strong and sure. His bewilderment was unsettling.

But, then, there was what he had said, and that made her heart sing.

She wanted to tell him she loved him so badly that she could taste the words in her mouth. But she couldn't say them. She didn't dare. He didn't want to hear them. The time might come—she allowed herself to think it for a single minute before pushing it out of her mind—when he wanted those words the same way he wanted her body. Until then, she could only do the second best thing, which was to love him out of his mind with her mouth, her hands and the body that he'd trained for the purpose so well.

THERE WAS NO rescue plane. There was no cruise ship, no sailboat, no charter. They had been on the island for ten days, and even Spencer was having his moments of doubt. He tried to hide them from her, but she saw the worried look he sometimes got when he sat on the beach gazing out to sea, with his legs bent and his elbows on his knees. She had stopped asking about it, in part because he never admitted to concern, in part because she didn't *want* him to admit to it—because the rest of their time was heavenly.

Jenna had taken vacations before, but never one like this. Neither of them wore a watch. They woke in the morning when they were rested, and went to sleep at night when they were tired. Their days were filled with walking, swimming and sunning. They read a lot; between the books Spencer had brought and those Jenna had packed, there was no shortage, particularly since their tastes were similar enough for them to exchange favorites. Occasionally they listened to his battery-operated cassette player, though they both agreed that the island's natural music was preferable.

As far as the necessities went, they were faring better than she'd ever have expected. They had gone through first the fresh food Spencer had brought, then the frozen things that had slowly defrosted in the cooler. They were into canned and freeze-dried food now, of which the latter's presence had surprised her. Spencer told her that he used freeze-dried foods in his travels and that the best source for them was located in New York, which was why he'd had a supply along. She thought it a fortunate coincidence. The freeze-dried foods, which were packed in boilable bags, were meals in themselves. He had enough to last them through a month of steady eating, and they weren't even eating them steadily. Once a day, Spencer waded into the water on the end of the island that was banded by a shallow reef and caught fish. He cleaned them and cooked them. Jenna had never tasted anything as fresh or as good. Some of this she knew was due to the island ambiance. She felt part of the environment there, one more living creature struggling to survive.

No. Not struggling. Spencer had been right about that. They had food and shelter. They were in no danger. Indeed, worry about rescue notwithstanding, she was having the time of her life. She knew the island now, so that even those parts she had once considered shabby had taken on beauty. And then there were those spots that had been beautiful from the start.

The waterfall was one such place. It was located at the highest point on the island. They had discovered it the second day they were there, when they had followed the stream up the hill to where it first gurgled out through large rock formations. And a more Edenic spot Jenna couldn't have imagined. The trees were high and green here, the ground carpeted with moss. The rocks were smooth, some tall, some flat, and the water that spilled over the highest of them was more gentle and refreshing than any shower she had ever stood under. They had taken to climbing the hill at the end of each day, not only to clean themselves of the salt and the sand that clung to their bodies, but to watch the sun settle slowly into the ocean.

On this day, Jenna particularly enjoyed the curtain of water that fell from her hair to her shoulders and over her body. She had woken that morning feeling muzzy, and as the day had progressed, the heat had bothered her more than usual. Now, letting the soap stream off her, she felt renewed.

Spencer had finished his own shower. He was faster at it than her on even the best of days, but he never hurried her along. Rather, when he was done, he stretched out on the largest and flattest of the rocks and watched her. In time, she joined him. She wiped her face with a towel while he made a gentle twist of her hair and squeezed the water from it.

"If you have a daughter, she'll have hair just like this. Do you ever think about that? Do you ever picture what our child will look like?"

Jenna didn't immediately answer. The "our" reverberated in her mind. He hadn't used it before, not in any of the other questions he had asked. And he had asked. For a man who proclaimed to want nothing to do with a baby, Spencer had developed a puzzling interest in Jenna's. But he hadn't said "our" before.

It was like the phrase "having sex," she mused. Somewhere along the line, that had become "making love," and it made sense, since she was in love. But Spencer had used the term first, and he wasn't in love— or if he was, it was a love that came in a far second to his work, which was the love of his life.

She pictured him going off in November to salvage his Spanish galleon. Then she pictured him going off the following year to explore something else. By then the baby would be born. She pictured it, too, and felt a pulse of serenity.

"Curls," she said. "I had curls when I was little. Boy or girl, it'll have curls. And, yes, dark hair. We both have that. Likewise, skin the color of cream."

"I don't have skin like that."

"You do."

"Where?"

She turned her head and eyed him boldly. "Your groin."

"You've been observant."

"Uh-huh." Actually "observant" didn't begin to explain what she'd been. She suspected she knew Spencer's body better than she knew her own. She could certainly see most of it more easily, particularly when he stretched out and let her look, which he did often.

The only rule he had was that she not stop at looking. She hadn't broken it once.

Now he frowned. "If it's a girl, she'll be a knockout. Guys will be after her all the time. You'll have to be careful, Jenna. I know what guys do. I was damned randy when I was a kid."

"When you were a *kid?*" she murmured facetiously. If he heard, he didn't let on.

"Everyone talks about safe sex, but kids still think they're immortal."

Jenna couldn't think years ahead, when she had so much to go through first. She blotted the rest of the water from her body, then reached for the lotion she always carried. He had laughed the first time she'd done it, telling her that body lotion was totally out of place at an island waterfall, but he'd been the one to remind her to take it the next time they'd gone.

"It's tough raising a child these days," he went on. "Even in a two-parent family. Are you sure you'll be able to do it alone?"

"Uh-huh." She rubbed the lotion into her legs, squeezed out more and applied it to her stomach.

"Babies are totally dependent. They need constant care. Won't it be tough on you?"

"No tougher than on any new mother."

"How will you go places with it? Babies cry at the drop of a hat."

"They cry if they're tired or hungry or wet. I'll make sure mine isn't any of those things—at least, not for long and not if I'm taking it somewhere." She spread lotion on her shoulders.

"Will you put it on your back in one of those carriers?"

She grinned. "That sounds like fun."

"But how will you manage it? Don't you need two people to get it up there?"

She looked at him again. "Do you need help putting *your* pack on your back?"

"No."

She arched a brow, then returned to lotion her arms, but her thoughts remained on his questions. Something was going on in his mind. If he was trying to suggest that she needed a husband, he was barking up the wrong tree. If he was trying to convince himself that babies were more work than they were worth and he was therefore right in wanting no part of them, he wouldn't get any encouragement from her. And if he was trying to discourage her from having the baby at all, it was a little too late.

"You can't have a baby where I go," he declared.

She kneaded lotion into her hands.

"You can't have a *woman* where I go," he added.

She drew dabs of cream from between her fingers.

"Sometimes I'm miles from civilization," he continued piously. "There aren't any phones, there aren't any baths, there aren't any beds."

Jenna could have sworn he was trying to justify his lack of a wife and family, but what he described was nothing different than what they had here. Granted, she wasn't his wife, but she wasn't minding life here. She hadn't complained once.

"If you get sick," he argued, "you can't run to the drugstore for an antihistamine. You can't run to a restaurant for dinner if you get tired of cooking. You can't go to a movie if you're bored, or run to the bookstore for something to read."

"That sounds like a very difficult life," Jenna said.

"It *is* difficult. There are days when I trek miles and miles with a heavy pack on my back. A woman couldn't do that, much less with a baby." He snorted. "I can just see you stopping in the middle of the tundra to nurse." He went still. "You are planning to nurse, aren't you?"

"Yes."

"Well, you can't nurse where I go. We rough it out there. We're often on the go twelve hours a day." He snorted again, louder this time. "Can you even begin to imagine what that kind of life would be like for a woman at the end of her pregnancy?"

Quietly, she answered, "I can't begin to imagine what *any* kind of life would be like for a woman at the end of her pregnancy, since this one's my first." The words were barely out, when her heart began to thud. She wondered if she'd given herself away. Had he caught it?

When he didn't answer, she glanced over her shoulder. He looked troubled. Her heart beat louder.

"Are you frightened?" he asked.

"Frightened?"

"Of the last month."

She let out a tiny breath. "A little."

"I wonder how big you'll get." He reached for her arm and drew her around. His eyes touched her breasts, then fell to her stomach. His hand followed. He rubbed his knuckles over the soft skin below her navel. His voice was a gritty whisper when he said, "There were pregnant girls in that Indian tribe I studied. They wore no more clothes than anyone else, so you could see their bellies. Sometimes, an elbow or knee poked at them from inside. I used to be fascinated by that." His hand slid lower, knuckles brushing the spot so close to where

Jenna's baby would emerge. "They let me watch a birth once. It was incredible."

Jenna swallowed. Her heart had swelled to twice its normal size, which was why she said without thinking, "You could watch the birth of our baby if you want to."

His hand came to a gradual stop, then fell away. He flattened it on the stone, straightened his shoulders and raised his eyes to hers. "The agreement was that I'd make you pregnant. That's all."

She was stung. Quickly, she said, "I know, and I can do just fine on my own, but you said that you found watching a birth to be incredible, so I thought—"

"Just think pregnant." He rose to his feet. "When will you know?"

She forced away her hurt. "Five days. Or six." She wasn't sure. Keeping track of the time had become difficult. One day blended into the next.

He nodded and turned away to scoop up his towel. Without waiting for her to join him, he started back down the hill.

JENNA AWOKE the next morning feeling nauseous. It passed as soon as she'd had breakfast, so Spencer knew nothing of it. She was infinitely grateful for that. He hadn't been in the best of moods when they'd returned to the plane the night before, and though he held her closely through the night and seemed calmer this morning, she didn't want to risk setting him off again.

The nausea returned late that afternoon. She snacked on a handful of crackers. That helped.

The following morning, though, she wasn't as lucky. Again she awoke nauseous. Ignoring it only worked until she left the cover of the tarp and was headed for the latrine. Halfway there, she turned off the path and lost the contents of her stomach in the woods.

Spencer was on the path when she returned. "What's wrong?"

"I'm not feeling great," she said. Passing him, she went quickly back toward the beach, wanting only to bathe her face and rinse out her mouth.

He was right behind her. "Did you throw up?"

"Yes."

"Was it something you ate?"

"I don't know."

"Did you feel sick during the night?"

"No."

She broadened her stride on the sand. When she reached the water, she sank to her knees and immediately scooped a handful of water to her face.

He hunkered down beside her. "Jenna?"

"Give me a minute," she murmured weakly. She was still feeling queasy, though there wasn't anything left in her stomach to heave.

"It's too soon to be morning sickness, isn't it?"

She didn't answer. She was weak and suddenly tired of keeping the secret.

"Isn't it, Jenna?"

"I don't know."

"You said morning sickness wouldn't begin until five or six weeks at the earliest. You told me that before you went to Hong Kong, remember?"

She nodded. The water was helping. She scooped more to her forehead, her mouth, the back of her neck.

"If you became pregnant while we were here, you'd only be a week and a half along."

"Maybe this is an aberration."

"Maybe you were pregnant before you stepped foot on my plane. That would explain why your breasts were bigger than I remembered them feeling."

She splashed her face one last time and hid behind her hands.

"Jenna?"

She didn't know what to say.

"Damn it, Jenna," he growled in warning, then with dawning awareness. "It's true, isn't it?" He took her wrists and pulled her hands from her face. "Are you pregnant?"

12

JENNA COULDN'T LIE. Not anymore. "Yes, I'm pregnant," she said, and kept her eyes wide on Spencer's to gauge his reaction.

He looked at her stomach, swallowed and looked back up. "It happened in Washington?"

She nodded.

"But you *denied* it."

"I know."

"*Why?*"

She could have lied again and said that she hadn't been sure she was pregnant, but she ruled out that thought in a second. She wasn't a deceitful person. She hadn't wanted to lie in the first place, but she'd seen no choice. Now the dismay on Spencer's face gave her pain. It was time for the truth. "I was selfish," she said, feeling the burden of her guilt. "I wanted to be with you again. I knew it would be the last time, and thought there wouldn't be any harm done."

"No *harm* done?" he bellowed. In a flare of the temper that Jenna knew existed but had been so rarely directed at her, his face was suddenly darker, his hands tighter around her wrists. "You came on my plane knowing that you had a mortal fear of it, knowing that the flight would be traumatic—"

"Not traumatic—"

"Frightening enough so that you might have lost the baby."

"I didn't lose the baby. I never thought I would."

"You didn't say anything when we landed. You let me go on thinking you weren't pregnant. I led you up and down, all over and around this island. I had you walking in the rain and sleeping on the ground and eating dried biscuits and freeze-dried beef, and through it all, you kept your mouth shut, when you should have been home seeing a doctor and eating fresh food and taking vitamins." His fingers dug into her skin. "I thought you *wanted* this baby."

"I do," she cried, "I *do*." Tears sprang to her eyes. "It's the most precious thing in the world to me!"

"If that's so, *why didn't you tell me you were pregnant?*"

"Because it wouldn't have changed anything!" Defensively, she explained, "There was nothing wrong with my climbing all over the island or walking in the rain or sleeping on the ground or eating what I ate. Those things are all fine—I've made sure they are. But if I'd told you the truth, you'd have been angry and worried, just as you are now, when there's no point! All the anger and worry in the world won't get us off this island! Your plane won't fly! You can't *change* that, Spencer!"

He stared at her long and hard. Finally, in a defiant voice, he said, "I sure as hell can."

She didn't understand, but before she could ask what he meant, he had dropped her wrists and was stalking across the sand, headed straight for the plane. When he was halfway there, he did an abrupt about-face, returned to where she still knelt and took her hand. "Come on. We're packing up."

"Now?"

"We're leaving." He drew her up and set off. His grip was firm, his voice tight.

"But how?" she asked, confused.

"My plane."

"You need parts."

"Not by a long shot."

"But you said we couldn't fly without them."

"I lied."

"*What?*"

"I lied."

She dragged her feet in the sand. "Lied how?"

"There's nothing wrong with the plane. We can fly."

"Nothing wrong?"

"That's right."

"No electrical problem? No *radio* problem?"

"Nope."

"I don't believe you."

"Believe what you want. You're going to have something to eat while I dismantle this camp. Then we're taking off."

She was still trying to grasp what he'd said. For eleven days they had been marooned on an island waiting for rescue. Or so she'd thought. "We're leaving, just like that?"

"I want you back in Rhode Island where everything is safe and predictable. I want you seeing your doctor. Hell, prenatal care is all you read about nowadays."

Jenna didn't give a damn about prenatal care just then. "You *lied* to me, Spencer?"

"Yeah, I lied."

Furious, she pulled her hand from his and took a step away. "You planned this accident, knowing that my parents died in one just like it? How *could* you?"

He climbed aboard the plane and called over his shoulder, "It was about time you got over that fear. Besides, there wasn't any accident. I kept telling you I knew what I was doing. Our landing here was a carefully planned maneuver."

"But we landed on a beach!"

He was rummaging in the food boxes. "I've landed on this beach dozens of times. The island is owned by a friend of mine. He knew we'd be here. That's why no one else dropped by."

Her fury rose. "You knew we wouldn't need a bonfire? You knew we wouldn't need your flare gun? You knew no one would come looking? I'll bet you even told Caroline where we were going!"

"Sure did. I didn't want anyone up there worrying." He emerged with a juice box and tossed her one. She caught it on reflex and angrily threw it back. It missed him, hit the door and fell to the ground.

"All those supplies—you bought them with this in mind." Not coincidence at all, but careful planning. She should have known. She'd read every one of his books. He planned his adventures well. "You had just enough fresh food to be eaten before it spoiled, just enough ice packs to keep the frozen food frozen until the fresh food was gone. You had soap and towels and toilet paper. You had books and a cassette player. You even had sun block."

"So did you," he said, and retrieved the juice box.

"Of course I did. I thought I was going to the Keys!" The extent of his deceit cut her to the quick. "I should have guessed. It was too pat. But I trusted you!"

"The way I trusted you."

"Hold on, Spencer. There's a difference. I never actually lied. I never actually said I wasn't pregnant. I misled you, and then I didn't correct you when you assumed I wasn't. But you—you contrived an entire story, one outright lie after the next. That's *indefensible*."

He handed her a chocolate-covered breakfast bar—which he had previously claimed he'd brought along because he loved munching on the things at home. "Eat this. And the juice."

She ignored the offering. "How *dare* you do this to me, Spencer! How *dare* you decide I should get over my fear of flying! How *dare* you take my entire life in your hands without giving me a say!"

"Oh, please," he muttered, then said more loudly, "take the food, for God's sake."

"I don't want it. I want to know how long you were planning to keep me here."

His dark brows were drawn tightly together. "You sound like it was a prison. Were you unhappy? Were you mistreated?"

"I was deprived of the freedom to leave."

"Did you want to leave?"

"That's not the point. The point is that I had a right to know the truth!"

His eyes drilled hers. "So did I!"

"You'd have known the truth when I missed my period," she said, feeling suddenly defeated. Her stomach was starting to churn again. "All along I knew I'd be telling you then. So when did *you* plan to tell *me?*"

"Long before now, I gotta say." He smirked. "I never thought you'd last here. I thought you'd be tearing your hair out after a week. I thought you'd be sick of the sand, sick of the bugs, sick of the heat. You've been a trooper, angel." He held out the food. "Take this."

"I don't want it!" She turned away. "I feel sick." Not knowing what else to do, she walked down the beach to the same rocks she'd sat on that very first day. She'd been feeling highly emotional then. She was feeling highly emotional now. And nauseous.

Spencer came up from behind and reached around to offer her a handful of crackers. "I should have known what was up when you were munching on these things," he grumbled. "How many days have you been feeling sick?"

"Two."

Swearing under his breath, he nudged the crackers at her hand until she finally took them. Then he went back to the plane.

For several minutes, Jenna stared at the crackers. She felt miserable. They would help her stomach, but she didn't know what would help her mind. She didn't have to look back to know that Spencer was packing the plane. He was taking her home. Their time together was over.

Tucking her face to her knees, she began to cry. Deep, soft sobs welled from within. She wanted to stop— Spencer hated tears—but the emotion behind them was too strong. So, hugging her legs, she let them come. In time, they eased. Hiccuping, she turned her cheek to her thigh and looked out to sea.

It would be good to go home, she told herself. It would be good to have a hot bath, to brush her hair until it was smooth, to put on real clothes. But Lord, she'd miss Spencer. All along, she had known love might be a problem, but she had underestimated its scope. Forgetting him was going to be impossible. She would see him every time she passed the room he'd slept in at her house, every time she watched a movie on television, every time she read a book or ate a piece of steak or saw an airplane, every time she kissed his baby good-night. Letting him go was going to be like severing a part of her heart. Already she felt the pain.

Her throat tightened into another knot. She swallowed, forcing its release. Taking a full breath, she straightened. Crying wouldn't accomplish anything. She was an accommodator. Life went on. She would survive—more than survive—do well. After all, she had a baby coming.

Who wanted an adventurer, anyway? Adventurers might be exciting, but they wouldn't be around when you wanted them most. They'd be off chasing dreams of their own. Besides, they were scheming, bald-faced liars.

Slowly she ate one cracker, then a second. Crumbling the remaining few in her hand, she tossed them toward the water for the terns that dove nearby. She pushed herself from the rock and went to the water's edge to cleanse her face of the ravages of her tears. Then, knowing that the next few hours would be the most painful of her life but that they had to be endured, she went to join Spencer at the plane.

He was nearly ready. The tarp was down, the towels and blankets stowed, those personal effects that had been lying on a makeshift table of driftwood cleared off and packed. The beach that had been their little home looked so tragically bare that Jenna felt the threat of tears yet again, but she refused to let them flow. Life was full of heartache, she told herself. She'd get past this. She would.

"Are you less nauseous?" Spencer asked with a scowl.

"Yes."

"Then eat these." He handed her a banana and a single-serving bag of granola.

She didn't want to talk or argue or do anything that would prolong the agony of their parting. The sooner she was back in Rhode Island, the better. So, though she had no intention of eating, she took the food.

He stood watching her with his hands on his hips, seeming to know exactly what she had in mind. "Go on."

"I'll eat while you pack."

"I'm done. Eat before we take off."

He was nagging. She didn't like it. "Have you eaten?"

"I'm not hungry."

"Well, neither am I."

"Eat for the baby, then."

"I'll eat for the baby later," she snapped, thinking how impossible overbearing men could be. "I don't *feel* like eating now."

"Some mother *you're* gonna make."

"And what difference is it to you? You didn't want this baby to begin with. You didn't want the responsibility. So I'm telling you not to take it. Let *me* worry about the baby."

He stared at her then, and his eyes shook her. She'd seen anger in them before, but she'd never seen the kind of cold fury that turned the silver in them to ice. She felt the chill all the way to her toes.

It was just as well, she reasoned, though her heart broke a little bit more. She and Spencer could never be just friends again. Their feelings were too strong for that. If they couldn't love each other, they'd have to hate each other—a tall order on her part and one she would have to work at, but it was the only way. The only way.

As though he had reached the same conclusion, Spencer gestured her into the plane with an angry toss of his head. He climbed in after her and strapped himself in, then started flipping switches. In no time the propellers started to turn.

"You bastard," she muttered.

"Yup."

She clamped her teeth together and stared blindly ahead. She didn't look at Spencer when he maneuvered the plane to the end of the beach and turned around. She didn't look at their camp when they accelerated past it. She was too heartsick to be frightened when the wheels left the ground and the plane slowly rose into the air.

All she wanted was to go home. It would be an hour and a half to Savannah, then two and a half to Rhode Island. She willed the time to pass quickly. After a few minutes, in hopes of helping it along, she looked out the side window.

"What's that land mass?" It extended forward and back for as far as she could see and looked suspiciously like the mainland.

"Florida," he said tersely.

"If we're heading north, what's it doing on my side of the plane?"

"We're heading south."

"But I live north."

He didn't respond to that other than to clench his jaw, which made his profile even harder than it already was. He was more tense than she'd ever seen him, and angry, very angry. Well, Jenna thought, so was she, and she didn't like what she was reading between the lines. "I thought you were taking me home."

"I am."

"To *my* home."

He flexed a muscle in his jaw, which looked tight enough to snap.

"Enough, Spencer," she declared, sitting ramrod straight behind her seat belt. "You decided we'd go to that island, so we went. Now it's my turn to decide, and I decide that you deliver me back to Rhode Island."

"I'm not flying all the way up there now," he snapped.

"Why not? You have nothing better to do until November. You told me so yourself."

"I have to think. I need time. I don't know what to do."

"I'll tell you what to do. Fly me to Rhode Island, drop me off and let me be."

"I can't do that."

"Why not?"

"Because we're not finished."

Jenna felt the slow twist of a screw inside her. The pain was unbearable. "We are—we are! You did your part. You gave me my baby. There is nothing else you have to do. I signed papers to that effect."

"Well, *I* didn't sign any papers!" he thundered. "And you can take yours and burn them, for all I care! They don't mean squat to me!"

Jenna stared at him in disbelief.

He went on angrily. "I *told* you I was going to have trouble with this. I *told* you I couldn't father a child and not care about it. I warned you, Jenna, but you seemed to feel that those papers were some kind of protection. Well, they're not! I can't just ignore the fact that my baby's growing inside you. I can't just go off and forget it. Hell, don't you think I wonder what it looks like, too?" He drove a hand through his hair. The other was white-knuckling the throttle.

Jenna was afraid to think ahead.

"Yeah, I planned this trip," he went on. His eyes were focused on the horizon. His tone was one of brassy self-mockery. "I thought to myself, okay, Spence, the woman turns you on. She was real easy to be with in Little Compton. She was real easy to be with in D.C. She should be real easy to be with in the Keys. Then I thought about the island, and I thought, what an adventure! She's used to marble and velvet. Let's see what she makes of seaweed and sweat." He added softly, "I didn't fool myself too much. Sure, I wanted to see if you'd crumble, but in the meantime I wanted to enjoy you. And it wasn't just the sex. It was the being together."

He pursed his lips. His nostrils flared when he took a breath. "That's been driving me nuts, the being together. The *enjoying* being together. The looking *forward* to being together. I've never felt that for another woman, and I didn't want to feel it for you. But I went ahead and made plans to maroon us for a couple of weeks on the island because I couldn't resist. And was it ever fun buying supplies! I felt like I'd been gathering knowledge for years and was finally putting it to good use for the very first time. Can you imagine that?"

He sounded as if he couldn't. Jenna pressed her fingertips to her mouth.

He swore softly and shook his head. "Hell, it was good. Everything about it was good. I mean, you didn't crumble. You didn't complain. You were having just as much fun as I was, and you were doing it in my kind of style." His voice faltered. "I don't think I'll ever forget the way you looked sitting there in the surf with nothing on but your bikini bottoms and my baseball cap. I mean, talk about tugging at heartstrings." He swore again, and she thought she saw something wet and glimmering in his eyes. "I could've stayed there forever. Do you know that? I don't think I've stayed anywhere for more than six months in the past twenty-three years, but I'd have stayed on that island forever. Or at least until we'd run out of food." He grunted. "Or until you'd gotten pregnant. Boy, it didn't take long, did it?"

Jenna wanted to speak, but her throat was too tight. Her heart was wedged there, along with her hopes and dreams.

"And now I don't know what in the hell to do," he sputtered. "Okay, so I've got you off the island and on your way back to civilization, but if that means I won't see you again, I can't do it—I just can't do it. I feel too much. I want too much. I can't just drop you back there and fly off, and only some of that has to do with the baby. Most of it has to do with you. When we were making love, I wasn't thinking of the baby. When you told me you weren't pregnant last month, I was disappointed for you but not for me. I wouldn't have been upset if we'd had to keep trying for months, because it would have given me time to figure things out. But you're pregnant now, damn it. So I don't have that time. And I don't know what to do."

Jenna was daring to hope. "What do you *want* to do?"

He shot her a terrified look. "Marry you. Have you ever heard anything so crazy? I mean, here I am running all over the world, and I want to marry you. I want you legally bound to me. I want to know you'll be waiting when I come home. I want to send you flowers again, and rub sunscreen on you again, and carry your shoes and your bags and your books. I want to knot my tie around your hair again. I want our kid to have my name." He shot her another look, no less terrified than the first. "But you don't want any of that, and I don't blame you. You're a capable woman. You have your own corporation, your own house and now your own baby. You don't need me." This time when he looked at her, he scowled. "Put that back on, Jenna."

She had unbuckled her seat belt and was climbing toward him. When her bottom touched his thigh, she wound her arms around his neck. "You're wrong, you're wrong, you're wrong," she whispered, and started to cry. "I do . . . need you. So . . . much."

"Oh, God, don't cry. Jenna, please." His voice broke. "You don't know what that does to me." He wrapped an arm around her and held her convulsively close.

"I love you," she sobbed.

"Oh, God."

"I do...and I lied about something else. Back on the island . . . I said that the baby was . . . the most precious thing in the world to me. It isn't true—it was once, but it isn't anymore. You're . . . just as precious to me as the baby. . . but I can't hold you back, Spencer. If I did, you'd resent me the way you resent your parents. That would *kill* me."

His arm tightened around her. "Oh, Jenna."

"I love you," she whispered. Now that she'd said it, she couldn't say it enough. "I love you."

He let out a ragged moan. "Ahh, angel." The hand that was wound around her pulled her hair back from her ear so that he could put his lips there. In a tortured whisper, he said, "I don't want to be living out child-hood fantasies when I'm old and gray. I want life to hold more than Spanish galleons, sparkling gold and sex."

"I was *awful* to say those things."

"You were right to say them."

"But your life is terrific."

"It's not enough. I keep running so I don't miss things, but I miss them, anyway. I want warmth, angel. I want a home."

Jenna had never thought to hear those words. Her tears came again. "What should we do?"

"Think. We should think. And you should sit down and put that seat belt back on. You're making me nervous."

"I trust your flying."

"Yeah, well, you may not in a few minutes if you don't strap yourself in. I'm feeling the need to do more than hold you."

"Oh." She drew her head back and looked up at him. "But nothing's been settled.

He kissed the tears from her cheeks. "One thing has." His voice was heart-stoppingly tender, as achingly warm as the silver in his eyes. "There's love here. Somehow we'll find a way to make things work."

FOR AS LONG AS HE LIVED, Spencer would never believe how simple it was, but that was because, never having been in love before, he hadn't known its power.

Jenna had insisted on passing the presidency of McCue's to her vice president. Spencer protested, but she claimed that she would likely have done it, anyway, once the baby was born. She wanted more time for her family, she said, and besides, she was still chairman of the board, and the company's controlling stockholder.

They were married on the Thanksgiving weekend. Spencer's parents were pleased as punch with the union—then appalled when Spencer promptly took

Jenna to the South Seas for three months. Even Caroline was miffed, complaining that instead of regaining a brother she was losing a sister-in-law. But Jenna had insisted on the trip. She had known Spencer wanted to go, had gotten full clearance from her doctor, and told anyone who argued that since Spencer had won his court case but was waiting to salvage his galleon until after the baby was born, this was *definitely* the time to go.

And Spencer thought *he* had wanderlust! She had been as enthusiastic as he every step of the way, ballooning belly and all.

Now, ballooning belly and all, they were back to await the birth. After spending time in Rhode Island to make sure all was well with McCue's, they had rented a cottage on the Maine coast, far enough from Spencer's parents to let him breathe, yet close enough to a top-notch hospital should the baby come early.

It was late March and still cool enough for Spencer to light a fire in the fieldstone hearth. With flames crackling around the logs, he sat on the floor, against the sofa. Jenna was straddling his lap. Her arms were looped around his neck; her eyes were level with his; a sweet smile softened her lips.

"You're a very handsome man, Mr. Smith," she said.

"Scar and all?"

She touched his jaw. "Scar and all."

"Did you know that was one of the first things I loved about you? You weren't fixated on the damn scar."

"It's just a scar. It's been part of you so long that I rarely notice it."

"Know how I got it?"

"Uh-huh. In a jeep accident in Kenya."

"Usually I tell women I was gored by an elephant."

"You don't."

"I do. It's more dramatic."

She rolled her eyes. "More drama I can do without." She grinned. "I still can't believe you're mine."

He took her hand to his mouth and kissed the diamond wedding band he'd so proudly given her. "I'm yours." Leaving her hand on his neck, he slipped his under her sweater. She was due in six weeks, but there were times when he wondered whether she would explode before then. Every bit of weight she'd gained was in her stomach, which protruded from her front like a great, fallen nose. From behind she looked as slim as ever, and he did enjoy her behind, but this was what he loved, this warm, smooth, tautly stretched belly that was glasslike and alive. "Feeling okay?"

She nodded. "Feeling great. I love it here."

"So do I. Maybe we could come back after the baby is born."

She shook her head. "We're going south. Your ship awaits."

"You're really looking forward to that, aren't you?"

"You bet. I've never worked with a salvaging crew before."

"Jenna, you're not working with my crew. How many times do I have to tell you that?"

"I know, I know. I'll be in your boat with a full-time captain aboard, but we'll be near the work boats, so I'll be able to see what's brought up. Are you sure your men won't resent my presence?"

Spencer wasn't sure of it at all. The boat he had bought for Jenna and him was far more luxurious than the one the men would be living on. Some envy was inevitable. If that envy reached an uncomfortable level in any of his crew, that man would have a quick, one-way trip to shore.

"My men will be fine. I'm the one who may have the problem."

"With resentment?"

"With distraction." His eyes widened. His voice dropped to an excited murmur. "It's moving. Whoa, feel that?" He had both hands on her stomach, fingers splayed to feel the nudge of a tiny arm or leg.

Jenna laughed. "Such wonder. Your expression is priceless. But you've felt that before."

"It's still the most incredible thing in the world." He kept his hands where they were. He liked thinking that the baby recognized his touch. He liked thinking that the most primitive form of bonding was taking place.

It probably wasn't. But he liked thinking it.

"Spencer?"

He looked up to find her eyes suddenly deep and intense. "What, angel?"

"I'm glad you're here."

"Where else would I be?" No other place in the world held half the challenge and a fraction of the reward.

"I mean, I'm glad you're doing this with me."

"I'm your husband."

"But you weren't my husband when I got pregnant, and I said I could do this alone. I think I was wrong. This wouldn't have been anywhere near as easy or exciting an experience if you hadn't been sharing it with me—"

He kissed her silent, then wrapped his arms around her and closed his eyes when she sighed in contentment against his cheek. He was always amazed to hear her say things like that, since *he* was the one who had been so wrong about being independent and self-sufficient.

Sure, he could be both. So could she. And they were fine things to be if one had to. If one didn't, ahh, that was where true joy lay.

Since he'd been with Jenna, even the smallest things in life had taken on new meaning. Her reaction was important to him. Her enthusiasm sparked his, and vice versa.

When he thought of traveling, he thought of ways he could do it with Jenna. And with the baby. The baby was coming along, too. He was thinking of spacing out his travels, actually. *Actually,* he was thinking of going back to school. He and Jenna had spent hours talking about his experiences with the Indians in the Amazon, and it had occurred to him that a degree in anthropology might be nice. It had occurred to him that if he went on for a doctorate, he might teach one day. He could intersperse classroom work with fieldwork. He could have a life that would be exciting and diverse, yet stable enough for a wife and child. And children.

He wanted all that. More important, Jenna wanted it, and her happiness meant the world to him. She was a treasure, fallen right into his hands. Now that he'd found her, he wasn't letting her go.

MILLION DOLLAR JACKPOT
SWEEPSTAKES RULES & REGULATIONS
NO PURCHASE NECESSARY TO ENTER OR RECEIVE A PRIZE

1. Alternate means of entry: Print your name and address on a 3"×5" piece of plain paper and send to the appropriate address below.

In the U.S.	**In Canada**
MILLION DOLLAR JACKPOT	MILLION DOLLAR JACKPOT
P.O. Box 1867	P.O. Box 609
3010 Walden Avenue	Fort Erie, Ontario
Buffalo, NY 14269-1867	L2A 5X3

2. To enter the Sweepstakes and join the Reader Service, check off the "YES" box on your Sweepstakes Entry Form and return. If you do not wish to join the Reader Service but wish to enter the Sweepstakes only, check off the "NO" box on your Sweepstakes Entry Form. To qualify for the Extra Bonus prize, scratch off the silver on your Lucky Keys. If the registration numbers match, you are eligible for the Extra Bonus Prize offering. Incomplete entries are ineligible. Torstar Corp. and its affiliates are not responsible for mutilated or unreadable entries or inadvertent printing errors. Mechanically reproduced entries are null and void.

3. Whether you take advantage of this offer or not, on or about April 30, 1992, at the offices of D.L. Blair, Inc., Blair, NE, your sweepstakes numbers will be compared against the list of winning numbers generated at random by the computer. However, prizes will only be awarded to individuals who have entered the Sweepstakes. In the event that all prizes are not claimed, a random drawing will be held from all qualified entries received from March 30, 1990 to March 31, 1992, to award all unclaimed prizes. All cash prizes (Grand to Sixth) will be mailed to winners and are payable by check in U.S. funds. Seventh Prize will be shipped to winners via third-class mail. These prizes are in addition to any free, surprise or mystery gifts that might be offered. Versions of this Sweepstakes with different prizes of approximate equal value may appear at retail outlets or in other mailings by Torstar Corp. and its affiliates.

4. PRIZES: (1) *Grand Prize $1,000,000.00 Annuity; (1) First Prize $25,000.00; (1) Second Prize $10,000.00; (5) Third Prize $5,000.00; (10) Fourth Prize $1,000.00; (100) Fifth Prize $250.00; (2,500) Sixth Prize $10.00; (6,000) **Seventh Prize $12.95 ARV.

   *This presentation offers a Grand Prize of a $1,000,000.00 annuity. Winner will receive $33,333.33 a year for 30 years without interest totalling $1,000,000.00.

   **Seventh Prize: A fully illustrated hardcover book, published by Torstar Corp. Approximate Retail Value of the book is $12.95.

   Entrants may cancel the Reader Service at any time without cost or obligation (see details in Center Insert Card).

5. Extra Bonus! This presentation offers an Extra Bonus Prize valued at $33,000.00 to be awarded in a random drawing from all qualified entries received by March 31, 1992. No purchase necessary to enter or receive a prize. To qualify, see instructions in Center Insert Card. Winner will have the choice of any of the merchandise offered or a $33,000.00 check payable in U.S. funds. All other published rules and regulations apply.

6. This Sweepstakes is being conducted under the supervision of D.L. Blair, Inc. By entering the Sweepstakes, each entrant accepts and agrees to be bound by these rules and the decisions of the judges, which shall be final and binding. Odds of winning the random drawing are dependent upon the number of entries received. Taxes, if any, are the sole responsibility of the winners. Prizes are nontransferable. All entries must be received at the address on the detachable Business Reply Card and must be postmarked no later than 12:00 MIDNIGHT on March 31, 1992. The drawing for all unclaimed Sweepstakes prizes and for the Extra Bonus Prize will take place on May 30, 1992, at 12:00 NOON at the offices of D.L. Blair, Inc., Blair, NE.

7. This offer is open to residents of the U.S., United Kingdom, France and Canada, 18 years or older, except employees and immediate family members of Torstar Corp., its affiliates, subsidiaries and all other agencies, entities and persons connected with the use, marketing or conduct of this Sweepstakes. All Federal, State, Provincial, Municipal and local laws apply. Void wherever prohibited or restricted by law. Any litigation within the Province of Quebec respecting the conduct and awarding of a prize in this publicity contest must be submitted to the Régie des Loteries et Courses du Québec.

8. Winners will be notified by mail and may be required to execute an affidavit of eligibility and release, which must be returned within 14 days after notification or an alternate winner may be selected. Canadian winners will be required to correctly answer an arithmetical, skill-testing question administered by mail, which must be returned within a limited time. Winners consent to the use of their name, photograph and/or likeness for advertising and publicity in conjunction with this and similar promotions without additional compensation.

9. For a list of our major prize winners, send a stamped, self-addressed envelope to: MILLION DOLLAR WINNERS LIST, P.O. Box 4510, Blair, NE 68009. Winners Lists will be supplied after the May 30, 1992 drawing date.

Offer limited to one per household.

LTY-H891

Coming Soon

Fashion A Whole New You
in classic romantic style
with a trip for two to Paris
via American Airlines®, a
brand-new Mercury Sable
LS and a $2,000 Fashion
Allowance.

Plus, romantic free gifts* are yours to
Fashion A Whole New You.

From September through November, you can take part in
this exciting opportunity from Harlequin.

Watch for details in September.

* with proofs-of-purchase, plus postage and handling

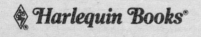